RUBIC'S RETURN

Book II, 'All the Sky' Series

Avalon Weston

'All the Sky' Series

I. The Running
II. Rubic's Return

Rubic's Return

Book II, 'All the Sky' Series

Avalon Weston

Published by
Glaston Hill

This book is a work of fiction. Names, characters, businesses, organisations, places, events, and incidents are either the product of the author's imagination or are used fictitiously. Any resemblance to actual persons, living or dead, events, or locales is entirely coincidental.

First published in ebook and print editions by Glaston Hill (Avalon Weston) in 2017.

British Library Cataloguing in Publication Data

A CIP catalogue record for this book is available from the British Library.

www.avalonweston.com

ISBN: (print) 978-1-9997197-0-8;

For MTM

Contents

The Creatures

The Foxes

Rubic: A fox seeking a purpose in life
Rubia: Rubic's mother, resident in Highgate Cemetery
Black: Rubic's father, the Leader at Highgate Cemetery
Butch: a curious fox and Rubic's brother
Pearl: his mate, a mysterious fox
Negruskic: a fox cub.

The deer

Caleb: an adolescent red deer stag
La Reine and her stag: fallow deer
Stella and the Mareschalle: red deer

The tigers

Turlough: moved from Dublin to the zoo in 2011
Soudari, Shouri, Svetti: three sisters, born in France

The badgers

Uncle Cousin: a long-lived resident of Highgate Cemetery

Brother Badger: called in to help the injured Rubic

The rabbits

Buckfast: a country rabbit – and others of his tribe

Mitty: a town rabbit, resident of Richmond Park

The cats

Charlie: an apprentice cat.

Gabrielle: a vicarage cat

Stefan: a church cat

The bats

Mercylargo – and his cloud

Other creatures

George: a magpie, reared by humans and unsure of his destiny
Anne: the last elephant in the UK to have performed in the circus
Hamlin: a brown rat
A buzzard
A Harris hawk
Dai: a red kite
A greater black-backed gull
The Rex: an escaped domestic ferret
Various stoats and weasels
Jendrix, a very senior ring-necked parakeet
Ned: a young ring-necked parakeet

Introduction

This is the second book in the series 'All the Sky'. The first book, *The Running,* told of the escape of the Seven Foxlings from the City to the new home they found for themselves up on the Moor, in the high country.

This journey came about when the foxes of the city forgot their history. They became too many. Year after year they had no Running. Their numbers grew and so the two-leggeds began to hunt them once more.

To save Blackberry, a fox who was seen by his tribe as special, seven young foxes left the city and undertook the longest Running there had ever been. The seven were Blackberry, Flutes, Butch, Rubic, Piana, Pearl and Troy.

They began new lives for themselves and found new ways of being. All but Rubic were happy in the high country. Rubic tried hard to settle in the hills. He watched his relations meet their mates and become content, but life on the open Moor was not for him. He found he couldn't kill other creatures, so in this wild country he went very hungry. Once snow began to fall on the Moor, his friend Caleb, the deer warned him, he wouldn't even be able to dig up worms.

As winter arrived even the blackberries died off. The City foxes had learnt to pick and enjoy the sweetness of these berries without ever getting prickles in their paws. Rubic's brother had taught them. That was how he got his name, Blackberry. The city foxes had in their turn shown the country foxes the trick of it. Sweet autumn blackberries were now a fox delicacy up on the Moor.

'In the city eating is simple,' thought Rubic. 'Food is just lying around in silver trays, simply waiting for me to find it.'

He had been told, many times by his mother that he was called Rubic because his favourite food was curry. In foxtalk, 'curry' is 'Ruby Murray'. As she would tell the story, his father had said 'We can't call him Ruby as he is a boy, so Rubic will do.'

The stories of the other six foxes who did the Running will be told in due time, but this book is the story of Rubic's return to the city and the adventures he had along the way.

1. On the Moor

Rubic was awake. He had watched all night. He was excited. Though it was still dark, he could see the lights of the seaside city below him. The sun was trying to creep over the purple cloud on the horizon. It wanted to reach the clear sky.

'Even here on the Moor,' he thought, 'the sun is caged, just like it was in the city.'

This sun was the weak, less determined sun of autumn. The beloved fiery fierce friend of the hot afternoons and long summer evenings had become frailer and less sure of itself. Nothing seemed certain anymore. Rubic knew winter was on its way.

All was quiet on the Tor. The partying had gone on most of the night. There had been races, leaping and jumping and tugs of war. There had been a telling of tales and much eating and drinking. It had been Rubic's farewell. Now everyone was asleep except Rubic himself.

He looked around him. Today was his day, he thought. Lately he knew he had not been a happy fox. He stretched out his neck and began grooming his pale red coat.

'I am going back,' he muttered as he combed through his fur with his teeth, removing all the twigs and burrs, the results of last night's partying. 'Today it will begin. They say I should carry the story of the Great Running back to the tribe. I will do that. But I want to find those four-leggeds with trees on their heads.'

Rubic was thinking of the red deer, with whom he'd become so enchanted, here on the Moor. He had heard talk that such a tribe existed near his city.

'If I could run with them there, like I did here …'

He remembered the magical experience as he continued to groom what should have been, but wasn't, a very lustrous brush.

'This dark place isn't for me. I'm glad for the others. They have found their mates and their way of being. But it isn't for me. No lights, no noise, so quiet. What happens? Ever?

Rubic was also a hungry fox and a growing fox. Even though he had eaten well last night, it had been the first time for many weeks. He still couldn't bring himself to kill and eat mice and voles and other small creatures as his fellow foxes did. His food had remained largely worms and blackberries. He was by no means the big fox he should have been.

This rather scrawny animal stood up and stretched, then, after looking around at the debris of the night before and at his sleeping relations, he quietly trotted down the narrow Tor path.

He was expected. At the bottom of the Tor stood the huge stag who was for the time being, Mareschalle of the Moor. Nearby in a tree perched the buzzard who had arranged this meeting and, hanging back a little stood Caleb, the Mareschalle's youngest son, who had become Rubic's friend.

The Mareschalle greeted him rather grandly, looking down at the pale orangish fox from his great height, for with his antlers he was perhaps seven foot tall.

'I hear you wish to know about our distant relatives,' he said. 'I will tell you what I know. I can see,' he said, eyeing the less-than-healthy-looking fox, 'my son is right. If you do not leave the Moor, you will be dead with the first snow and I owe you a debt.'

Caleb butted in.

'He knows that now. And we do owe him. Anyway, he is going back to his city, but he has heard tales, so have I, of places where two-leggeds walk among our kind and there are no guns.'

'Indeed. There is a story. Our kind have been in this land forever, but not in all of it. They say that many, many years ago, the two-leggeds came here and took a stag and some hinds from our Moor to this place you talk of. Their descendants live there still, together with the little Frenchies.'

'The little Frenchies?' asked Caleb.

'They are smaller than us and still have their own talk. They were brought over the sea in a ship so that the two-leggeds could hunt them. But they are small deer and the two-leggeds wanted bigger antlers to hang on their walls, so they came and took our ancestors to this place you talk of.'

'But they aren't hunted now?'

'No, just seen.'

'But are they free?' asked Rubic.

The Mareschalle looked at him and didn't answer.

'During the Running,' said Rubic, 'we met a pig and a horse and a cow, who were also just to be seen and not eaten. They were in what they called a City Farm, but they had never been free. They had always been tame creatures.'

'Leave it,' said Caleb. 'You won't get any answers. Those sort of words aren't our sort of words.' He turned to his father. 'Are there any more stories about our city cousins?'

'The only other thing I've heard,' said the big stag, 'and it is a very old story, is that those cousins of ours see themselves as special. They say they are the guardians of the grave of a two-legged King who died long ago in the north.'

It was clear to Rubic from the tone of the conversation that the big stag had no more information for him. The myths and legends of long ago were not going to help him find these creatures today. Having heard all that was going to be useful to him, Rubic, rather stiffly, nodded his head to the big stag and thanked him for his information.

'I will carry news of your tribe to your cousins, and Cheers Mate,' he said, using the formal words of the Creature Code.

'Good speed and a safe haven,' responded the big stag, giving the equally formal reply. Niceties having been completed, he wandered off towards his hinds.

Caleb remained.

'You ask difficult things. I don't think we need to know about this "free", do we? It don't concern us.'

Rubic couldn't help himself. He had to answer.

'Before we left the city there was much talk of this "free". There, they call the train tracks "the freedom road". You are free, but those sheep over there in that field are not.'

'But they are wild,' said Caleb. 'They are not tame, like the dogs in the houses or the birds in the cages.'

'I don't have the answers,' said Rubic, 'that's why I'm asking.'

Caleb looked at his foxy friend in exasperation.

'Anyway, what are you going to do next?'

Rubic knew that his city was a long way away. How to get there was his first question to himself.

He had to see Butch.

'I know who will have an idea', said Rubic to Caleb. 'My brother Butch. He got us here in the first place.'

It was true Butch had planned their journey from their city cemetery home to the railway station where they had stowed away on the train to Devon. The problem was how to find him. The last time Rubic had seen Butch he had been following another big bird as it led him to Pearl, the fox he hoped would become his mate. Rubic turned to the buzzard, who had been listening to all that had passed.

'Do you remember my brother?' he said. 'He went off with a Richard a bit like you, to find his cousin.'

'Indeed I do,' screeched the buzzard, in not an entirely friendly manner. 'That brother of yours and his mate really started something.'

Rubic looked puzzled and Caleb the deer turned his head to listen.

'You were talking of birds in cages. That bird you are talking of, that Richard, was hatched in a cage, and some say should still be there, but his mother made him escape. Then what happens? He meets your brother and that pretty little fox I carried over the hills.

She tells him he needs a mate and off he goes to chat up some of my cousins, down the road. I don't even know what those birds are doing living in the middle of the city anyway. It isn't the proper place for us buzzards. We are raptors and hunt across the hills.

The next thing we know is that this Texan hawk and one of my cousins are sitting on eggs and now there is a very odd-looking hawklet flying around town and sitting on the cliffs. Hmph!'

The buzzard's yellow eyes looked fiercely at the fox and the young stag. Rubic tried not to look too pleased. He knew he needed this bird's help. But he was glad. Butch and Pearl were building their own life and changing the world they had come to. He had a feeling that this was what all those who did the Great Running were supposed to do.

'But do you know where my brother and Pearl

are?' he asked.

'Aak! Yes,' screeched the buzzard. 'They have gone to live by the big water, you know, the sea. You can see it from the top of the Tor when the sky is clear.'

'You can,' said Rubic, 'and maybe he can,' he said, nodding at Caleb, 'but a fox like me close to the ground definitely cannot. How do I find them?'

'That's easy,' said the hawk. 'You just go south until you hit it. You can't miss the big water.'

'South?' said Rubic.

'City creatures! What can you do?' said the hawk. 'You will be going south if you make sure that the sun rises on this side,' he said, flapping his left wing, 'and sets on this side,' he finished, flapping the other wing.

'Look, that little fox Pearl, she was brave and she loved flying. For her sake, I will make sure a message gets to your relatives. They will be looking out for you. That OK?'

Rubic thanked the buzzard as hard as he could.

'Aaark,' was the reply. 'What happens, happens. Good speed then.'

With that the big bird spread its wings, flapped a couple of times, then lifted himself up, skirting the trees, swooping low over the moor, and rose up to disappear behind the Tor. Rubic's final 'Cheers Mate' was lost on the wind.

'So now you know more things and so do I,' said Caleb. 'But it is your time to go. If you find my cousins, tell them about us, here on the Moor.'

The young stag paused a moment.

'Cheers Mate,' he said and, tossing his head, set off to join the herd. He was a wiser young stag than he had been and one day he would find these new ideas to be of use. Rubic called his own formal farewell after him.

'And Cheers Mate to you too,' he barked.

The fox looked about him, then after carefully lining himself up with the rising sun on his left, lolloped off down the Moor.

2. Meeting With Family

Rubic found the going wasn't too difficult. For a while he was trotting along green paths on open moor, then between trees. Eventually he came upon a big grey road going south in his direction. He followed it keeping close to the trees at its edge. After a while he came upon a great flat place, which seemed to be where two-leggeds kept their tin boxes with wheels. There was a friendly smell.

'Aah,' he thought, 'I know what that is.' His nose followed it. It was more than friendly, it was delightful. It became stronger as he reached a metal frame with a plastic bag hanging from it.

'This is it,' he thought and, taking hold of the plastic between his teeth, pulled. The contents of the bag spilled on the ground around him.

'Heaven!' he muttered, gulping down the nearest thing. It was the remains of a ham sandwich. He knew that he only had moments before he was seen, so he grabbed another something, smelly, wrapped in paper, and headed off into the nearby bushes.

'Oy, Gerroff!' He heard the expected angry shout behind him.

Poking at his parcel, he found he had the remains of fish and chips. He wolfed it down.

'So good, so good,' he growled.

'I am a city fox,' he said to himself. 'This is my sort of food and the city is my kind of place.'

With a truly comfortable stomach, full of his sort of food, Rubic stretched out and thought about his future and his plans. He was also sure that the next thing he had to do was meet with Butch, his brother. Back in the city, among their tribe, before the Running, Butch made his fellow foxes somehow uncomfortable. He had been considered a bit weird. They were glad when he had got himself included in the Running. Rubic understood that. He knew Butch had ideas and that he saw more than most foxes and maybe more than most creatures.

With a full stomach, a clear head and more confidence than he'd had in months, Rubic was set to continue his journey south towards the sea. He was about to stand up and move on when he heard something.

First it was a two-legged shouting.

'Over there, over there, I tell you.'

'Look, in those bushes.'

'We'll get it. Dirty vermin.'

'Such a mess it's made.'

'In there, get him girl,'

There was a growl and the nearby bushes shook and parted. The largest canine Rubic had ever seen was standing there, snarling. It had a pointed nose, very large teeth and a very hairy coat. Luckily for Rubic, who was completely unprepared, it was still on a long lead.

The dog barked. Rubic leapt to his feet.

'Go on then. Let her off.'

The two-legged did as he was urged.

The long-haired Alsatian bounded at the fox.

Rubic ran. He ran right out of the bushes, across the flat grey space towards the fence on the other side. He could hear the dog howling behind him. The fence loomed up. He leapt at it, just managing to get his paws on the top wooden slat. With a struggle he was over the other side. He landed on his feet and looked behind him. The huge dog was barking fiercely at him, but from the other side of the wooden paling fence. It made no attempt to jump.

Rubic ran on uphill until he could disappear into the trees. There he paused and lay down to recover.

'Phew,' he thought. 'That was lucky. If he'd

got me, I'd have been in bits.'

He might have been wrong, because the dog was a guard dog rather than a hunter. Her job was to keep intruders out of her territory. It was, after all, Rubic who'd entered it and, in getting his food, managed to spread rubbish all over her clean car-park.

The two-leggeds seemed satisfied with the encounter.

'Well it won't be back in a hurry.'

'See we still need the Hunt though. That used to keep them out of the town.'

'Good girl, Bess, good girl. Good job.'

The Alsatian appreciated the pat and the praise.

It was a more wary Rubic who continued on his way. He crept on through the city, still going south. His nose recognised the salt in the air. It was the same salt smell of the 'big water' that all the foxlings' noses had met when they smelt it from the train on their journey from London. It had been Butch, of the seven, who had been most enchanted by the big water when he had seen it from the iron road.

Rubic pointed his nose to where the smell was strongest and followed it through the grey stone streets.

Suddenly, ahead of him he saw a mound of green grass rising up. He ran at the slope and, on reaching the top, found he was looking down yet another green slope with a very tall red and white tower in the middle of it. The green grass ended abruptly and beyond was the big water, the sea. The buzzard had been as good as his word.

Rubic found he was expected. Cautiously, he set off down the slope when there was a sudden rush of wind and a loud *Aaark!* A few feet in front of him, there landed a very large seagull with a fearsome-looking yellow beak. The bird and Rubic were about the same size.

The somewhat alarmed fox remembered the rules and interpreted the squawk correctly as 'Pax'.

'Fainites,' he growled rather nervously.

'Glad to know you city folk still know the old words,' said the bird. 'I was sent to show you the way to those other two of your kind.'

'Butch and Pearl?' said Rubic eagerly.

'Yup. But let's get a move on. This is the two-leggeds' special park. They don't like either of our species much and they are always here, watching.'

The great black-backed gull, for that was the name for his kind, began to strut towards a hedge at the side of the smooth green grass. Then he rose up and hovered.

Rubic understood what he had to do. Sure

enough, when he got to the hedge, low down, near the ground and barely visible, there was a gap and a faint path leading down the cliff.

He followed it down and down. He heard the noise of the sea get louder. He looked up and could see waves with their white crests rushing in towards him. He followed the track, which veered a little to the right and found himself at the beginning of what seemed to be a dark tunnel.

He paused.

From within came a yelp. Rubic recognised the voice and bounded forward into the darkness. The three foxes were delighted to be reunited. There was much nibbling and licking and yelping.

Rubic looked in surprise at his brother who seemed to have grown a lot, but he was amazed by Pearl.

When he had last seen this tiny fox, she had been very very sick and not expected to live. He had said the final fox farewell to her.

The words all foxes use are: 'We'll meet again'. They are understood to mean, 'in the fields of the ancestors'. It was unheard of ever to see again a fox to whom you'd said these words.

For this reason, Rubic found meeting her rather spooky. Especially now as her pale coat was lustrous and thick and she was only a little smaller than Rubic himself.

'But I said the words to her,' he said to Butch.

'Well I didn't,' said Butch. 'I knew she was a tough cookie.'

Nevertheless, Rubic felt that Pearl was a little mysterious and no longer the annoying little cousin she had been.

'You don't look so good yourself,' said Butch. 'We've got something special for you. Come on.'

Rubic followed the two foxes, as they led the way into what turned out to be a deep cave which went a long way back into the cliff. He saw Pearl jump up onto a broad ledge at the back of the cave and walk along it. Finally she turned around and sat down, looking expectantly at Butch. Somewhat puzzled, Rubic joined her. Pearl then in the manner of a conjurer whisked back a chunk of seaweed and Rubic saw a silver takeaway container.

'For you. Eat,' both the others barked.

Rubic sniffed. It was the old familiar smell of home, the dish for which he had been named. It was the remains of a curry, a tikka masala to be precise.

He ate. Afterwards, the three foxes settled on the ledge with Rubic in the middle. They set about comfortably grooming each other with the friendship of familiarity.

Finally the time came to exchange their stories.

Rubic told of his summer with the foxes of the Tor and how two more of the Seven Foxlings who had made the Running had started new lives. Flutes and Blackberry now had mates, he said, and were digging their own earths.

Pearl looked at him.

'You still can't kill creatures can you?' she said. 'That is why you are so thin.'

'That's why I have to go back to the city,' he said. 'I wasn't going to, but the Tor foxes said that when the snow comes and covers the grass there wouldn't even be worms and I would join the ancestors. There was an old grandmother there, Flora. She made me talk to the buzzard. He, by the way, sends his greetings to you, Pearl.'

He looked at his brother.

'It's you I need to see Butch.'

Rubic stopped telling his story and remembered his manners.

'What happened to you two? What is this place?'

'This is the same water we saw from the iron road,' said Butch. 'It goes everywhere, it moves in and out every day. It comes right up to here,' he said, looking down at the smooth sandy shore below the ledge on which the foxes were lying. 'It is so, so ... big. Anyway, it keeps us safe.'

'At first,' said Pearl, 'we were in this strange

dry place. That's where the other Richard, the one called a Harris hawk, who comes from Texas, lived. But now the two-leggeds have started digging with big machines so he had to move.'

'I've heard about him from the buzzard,' said Rubic. 'I'm not sure you are very popular there.'

'Oh?' barked Pearl. Rubic repeated the conversation he'd heard on the Moor.

'I'm so glad,' said Pearl. 'He was a lovely bird and didn't deserve to be an only. He helped us find this place. And I bet their chick will be amazing.'

'He is the one who told us the story that there were no foxes in this city. They had been chased away many years ago by two-leggeds in red coats they call the Hunt, so it seemed a good place to be. Food is easy and the big water brings new things to us every day. See,' said Butch pointing with his muzzle.

Rubic looked. Against the back wall of the cave was a strange collection of objects. Among the things to be seen were weathered white pieces of wood, a lump of tangled fishing net, and some thick blue rope. There was also the decaying remains of a dolphin and a green glass fishing float. Any passing two-leggeds would have been appalled at the smell coming from the fish and surprised by the green glass float. The fish had been dead some time and the skin was beginning to fall off its bones. Glass floats were rarely found washed up on beaches in these times, most having been replaced by orange plastic ones. Everything had been carefully arranged on the shelf.

'Why?' said Rubic.

'You remember those pictures on the wall of the tunnel in the place where all the animals were, where we rescued that Piana? Well it is something like that,' said Butch a little fiercely.

Rubic looked at Pearl. She looked back at him.

'It's important,' she said. 'I don't know why, but it is, especially that.' She went over and licked the green glass float, still in its netting bag.

Rubic had always known his brother was odd. This collecting of things proved it. He decided not to comment. But he had come to ask for help so he began.

'You had left us before we met the four-leggeds with trees on their heads ...'

'I saw something of them,' said Butch, 'from the trucks as they took us to the Moor.'

'Well,' said Rubic, 'Blackberry, Flutes and I warned their leader and saved him from a two-legged with a gun. Then we ran with the herd. It was wonderful, amazing. I can't explain it, but I need to be near them, those creatures with the trees on their heads. They don't kill to eat and they run like the wind.'

'And there are some back near our city,' interrupted Butch. 'That green bird told me about them.'

'I know and that's why I must go back. I will carry the news of our Running to the tribe, but I can also meet these creatures again. With them is where I should be,' said Rubic. 'That will be my place. But how do I get there? Can I get back on the iron road? Will that feline Sinbad help?'

'That won't work,' said Butch. 'There are no foxes around here, so sometimes I go and see Sinbad, for the news. He told me. Those big storms broke the iron road. It is being mended but the place is full of two-leggeds and big machines and not safe for creatures. We'll have to think of something else.'

Rubic felt defeated and it showed.

Pearl looked at him hard.

'What do you really really want?'

'I don't know,' said Rubic.

'Well maybe you should go and look until you find it,' she said. 'You can't go on like this, getting thin and being miserable. Is it a place or a mate you want?'

'I don't know,' said Rubic again. 'There is so much that doesn't have answers.'

'Like what?' said Butch.

'Why can't I kill things and other foxes can? They don't think it is wrong, like I do. Why couldn't I settle on the Moor? There was a lovely little fox there. She wanted to be my mate, and lots of other whys.'

'Like what?' said Butch again. 'It used to be me who asked that sort of thing. Now for me the answers are in that stuff.' He nodded towards the tangled collection on the ledge.

'Like why foxes are foxes and cats are cats and why the two-leggeds hunt us and why Richards can fly and we can't? Like why the creatures with trees on their heads can eat grass and be well but I get thin?

'Flora, that old fox on the Moor told me my job was to take our story back to the city, so I will do that, but only because I don't know what else to do.'

'At least that is something,' said Pearl. 'Maybe it is the journey you need to make. I flew with the Richard. I have seen trees and fields and long worms of water from far above. I know how little we are, but I also know how things are joined up. That is enough for me. But ... it is far, very far back to our city.'

'That is what you need, she is right,' said Butch decisively. 'I can see now. You need to seek and find your way. The buzzard showed you how to come south. Now you need to go east. That is where the sun rises. If you follow it you will get back to where we came from. Who knows what you'll meet on the road? There will be some answers. Anyway, we can show you where to start out and how to go east, to the old city.

'But not today. Today we show you our place. Tomorrow at sunrise we will show you the way back.'

For the rest of the day, Pearl and Butch showed off their new world. They showed Rubic how to play with the tide. When it was beginning to go out, they showed him how to search the sea weed at the high tide mark for anything useful. When it reached its lowest, they showed him how they made patterns in the sand and then watched as they were washed away as the sea came in.

They took him to a high rock where they could look out across the bay to a small island.

'See that,' said Butch. 'That green land. The big water goes all the way round it. We are going to go there one day. Pearl knows it can be done. She went on some smaller water on a wooden platform. We are going to find a way to go over there.'

Rubic was amazed that his weird silent brother had become so confident and happy and that the tiny sick Pearl had become this beautiful sleek vixen. He wondered for a little about staying with them, but he realised that in spring there would be cubs, and he had no mate and there were no more foxes in the city among whom he could find one. Somehow too, he knew he wasn't ready for the settled life of the earth, a mate and cubs.

The following morning at sunrise Butch and Pearl led him to the eastern side of their new city. They found a place under a tree, high up above the big broad road the two-leggeds called a motorway. All three foxes looked at the four-lane black tarmac snake stretching out as far as they could see. The other two had explained again to Rubic how the sun moved and how he could use it to show him his way.

'And keep away from those country canines,' said Pearl. 'Remember they aren't like the city poodles!'

'And if you are going to find dead food you will have to stay near to the roads, so remember the four-wheelers go much faster here than they ever did in our old city.'

There was a screech and a bird landed in the tree above them. Pearl looked up and then danced around with delight.

'Dai, Dai, Pax,' she called to him.

'Fainites,' replied the red kite, or that was what Rubic presumed he said, but the bird's

Welsh accent was so strong that he wasn't sure.

If Dai's yellow eyes could show affection, they did as he looked at Pearl.

'This is the other Richard who rescued me and took me into the sky,' she said and leapt up towards the branch on which the bird had settled.

'And you are no longer that sick little cub that I carried,' the bird replied. 'I couldn't carry you now!'

'What are you doing here?' asked Pearl.

'I told you I policed the motorways,' said Dai, the red kite. 'I had news, so I came to see what you very difficult foxes are up to now?'

They told him Rubic's story.

He put his head on one side and thought for a minute.

'You are right to follow my roads,' he said. 'They are dangerous, but there is always dead food. You just have to make sure you don't become that food. I will send messages.'

He looked at Pearl.

'You have changed things, girl. Probably good for us all.

Must fly now. Trouble at the turnpike.'

He paused and then as he flapped his wings and rose up into the sky, he rather more formally screeched 'Good speed to you. May you find a safe haven.'

'Cheers mate,' barked the foxes after him.

Pearl watched wistfully as he rose up into the sky.

'He is a special friend,' she said.

The three companions realised it was time for their farewells too.

'The words that Troy invented,' said Pearl, 'Until the Mela. We will see you again, I know. Find your way.'

'Until the Mela,' said Butch.

'Cheers Mate,' said Rubic and trotted off along the ridge of the motorway embankment.

Butch and Pearl watched him go.

3. A Solitary Road

Rubic trotted away along the embankment. He didn't look back.

It began to rain the big, solid, very wet watery raindrops that are common in the west of England. The sky was a heavy dark grey. Everything seemed bleak. His heart hurt. A two-legged would have recognised his feeling as loneliness. He wondered again if he should have stayed with Butch and Pearl, but he knew that in spring when the cubs came there would be no place for him.

The rain continued, if possible, heavier than before. Rubic didn't know what to do, so he simply moved steadily onwards to where he knew the sun should be. The rain, mostly, ran off his coat and dripped onto the ground, but Rubic's fur wasn't in as good condition as it should be, so the wet began to seep into his skin and bone. That was too much. Even his fur had stopped working.

'That's it,' he thought. 'I've had enough.'

He lay down on the grass and put his nose between his paws. This was it. He would cease to be. There was no point. He would just stay here and wait to join the ancestors. He shut his eyes and the raindrops continued to fall on his back and his head and his face. He was cold and numb. Eventually he slept.

He woke to feel the raindrops slacken off a little. He opened one eye and looked. It was still the same world. It was still grey and wet. There were no ancestors here. Nothing was easy.

His single open eye was caught by movement below him on the road. He opened the other and watched. Down there he could see the tin boxes of the two-leggeds whizzing along. He could see they went very fast. He watched a little longer and then fixed his eye on a big white box.

'I wonder if I can go faster than it does,' he thought.

He got up and watching the white box, began to trot. He tried to race parallel to the lorry, from where he was, high up. He ran and ran along the ridge of the embankment, but the white box never tired and never paused and was always ahead of him.

It was some distance before the exhausted fox collapsed in a heap. He watched the lorry continue relentlessly away from him.

'Well,' he said to himself, 'I suppose I've learnt something. At least I know there is no point trying to run with those things and they don't talk to you either.' He shook himself. 'And I'm not so wet now.'

The running had done its job. He had left the past behind. The ancestors would have to wait for this particular fox to join them.

Rubic was hungry. He remembered what the red kite had said. There would be dead food beside the road. He descended the embankment to the road side. As the vehicles rushed past he saw how very very dangerous they were. He understood now he could never have caught up with that white box on wheels.

Having decided it wasn't his time to join the ancestors, he became an extremely cautious scavenger. Carefully keeping all four feet firmly on the grass verge he followed the road. Sure enough, before long his nose told him there was food about. He came upon a carcase. It was a dead bird with long tail feathers.

'It has ceased to be,' he said firmly to himself. He pulled the remains into the bushes and ate. Then he groomed his wet coat and felt altogether better.

It was still raining when he'd finished, but there was now a lightness in the sky. Rubic headed up the ridge once more, to look towards it. In the distance he could see the beginnings of another city and arched over it was a rainbow.

Rainbows weren't new to him. They happened quite often on the Moor and even occasionally back in his old city and they were always seen by the foxes as a happy sign. Rubic shook himself and stretched. There was hope now. He set off towards the city he could see on the skyline.

It seemed to be quite a big city. He knew it wasn't his own. He decided he'd got to the middle when he found a flat green space, a tall grey-pointed building and lots of two-leggeds walking around. Some of them were all dressed in white and red and black and made up a long snake of people moving round the green. There was a man leading them carrying something golden which glittered in the morning light.

'Too many two-leggeds,' thought Rubic. He padded away from the procession, over the grass, under an ancient arch, along a street and then, having crossed a little bridge, found himself on the bank of a river.

It was a small, well-behaved, walled-in, city river, but nevertheless it was still living water. Its bouncing bubbling current cheered Rubic. He decided to follow it. There were big white birds swimming on it. He thought it was worth seeing if they would talk to him.

'Pax,' he barked at the nearest large white bird.

It stood up on its webbed feet, flapped its very large wings and sticking its neck out charged across the water at him, hissing fiercely.

Rubic took to his heels and ran as fast as he could along the riverside path.

'Well that didn't work,' he said to himself. 'I wonder what I did wrong?'

He was right to wonder. He had used the universal creature greeting and should have had the answer 'Fainites'. Sadly, not all peace treaties work all of the time.

His run had led him to a flat grey space covered with rows of big, long, wheeled boxes. He remembered they were the kind that held many two-leggeds and were soft and warm inside. Rubic had found the cathedral tourist coach park.

There was an unattended open door. Still shaken by his encounter with the swan, he leapt up the steps into the vehicle and looked around. He was about to settle on a soft cushioned seat, but then realised how quickly he would be discovered. He looked around again and saw a high shelf above the seats. That would be better, he thought. He jumped on a seat back and again onto the parcel shelf. He snuggled back into it and found, being a fairly small fox, he fitted well. He could look down on the whole coach and no one could see him.

He would have found it difficult to explain why he had got on the coach, but he knew that this box would go further and carry him faster than he could ever travel himself. After all, the Seven Foxlings who made the Great Running caught the train from Paddington Station. This wasn't so different.

He slept and then a couple of hours later, watched the coach fill up with two-leggeds. He wasn't at all sure he'd done the right thing, but it was done and he couldn't escape now. He put his paws over his nose and watched.

The two-leggeds settled into their seats. Someone reached up and put a bag on the shelf beside him, but the human wasn't tall enough to see onto the shelf so Rubic remained undisturbed.

One two-legged in the front talked to all the others through a stick in his hand, then some music came on and the coach set off.

The rhythm of the trundling vehicle lulled the fox. He was startled when a little over an hour later after a quick swerve it stopped. The door was opened and all the two-leggeds stood and lined up to get out.

When it was quiet and they had all got off, Rubic jumped down from the parcel shelf and trotted between the rows of seats to the door. He could see the human in charge talking to another, with his back to the coach door. There were bushes on the far side of the car park. In seconds Rubic was down the coach steps, across the concrete and into the bushes.

He wondered where he was. He pointed his nose in the air and sniffed. He was puzzled and sniffed again. He could smell strange creatures. His nose recognised the scent as something from before, back in his own city.

'The Zoo,' he thought. 'This place smells like that.' It was from the Zoo he and Butch had rescued Piana the Polish fox.

Rubic remembered and moaned.

'My Piana. She was so beautiful.'

She had been his first love. He thought her the most beautiful fox he had ever seen. She was a fur fox smuggled into England on the Eurostar train and she had spurned his love.

For a moment the feelings of lowness and despair returned, but only for a moment. The rainbow had done its work. Rubic was a young fox and there was a whole world out there. He could no longer be grabbed by the claws of depression.

He raised his head and sniffed once more. He trotted out of the bushes to the top of a little rise and looked out across green fields. He could see creatures. He looked again. They were very strange creatures.

'Long necks, little heads, but not deer,' he said to himself. 'They've only got tiny twigs on their heads.'

He realised there might be danger.

'Must watch out for two-leggeds and long guns,' he thought.

He slipped into a copse and crept along the treeline, keeping his eyes on the fields.

From behind him there came a long low growl.

He turned.

Far, far too close to him he could see three creatures much, much larger than himself and much larger than any canine he had ever seen. The three stood amidst the trees. The stripes on their coats made them hard to see. The nearest to him had its mouth still open and this time snarled directly at him. Their smell drifted on the breeze.

It was feline, not canine. He looked at their legs. Their feet were paws with pads like his own and with big claws, but each foot was almost the size of his head.

4.

The Grand Felines

Rubic froze. He understood that if he ran, instantly any one of these giants would be on him in a leap and those teeth would finish him off in a single bite.

'Pax, Pax, Pax,' he barked trying not to sound as scared as he was.

The nearest tiger, for that is what these large creatures were, paused in its growl and looked at the fox.

'Fainites,' it snarled, less fiercely. 'I haven't heard anyone use "The Word" for a long time. Where did you learn it? And we don't get many of your sort in here.'

Now the one thing Rubic had learned was that all creatures like to tell their own history to any new species they meet.

He had, in his travels, listened to the stories of black rats, brown rats, grey squirrels, several hawks and a green parakeet, so he knew how to answer.

'I come from a city where we all know the words and they are used quite often,' he said. 'There would be a lot of trouble otherwise. But sir, I have never met a feline like you before. Where do your kind come from?'

There were four tigers in this wood and the other three, sisters, sensing that there was a tale to be told, circled and settled themselves comfortably on a dry piece of ground. All four were watching Rubic.

He sighed a little with relief as those three at least, relaxed.

The largest tiger, the one who had growled at Rubic, remained standing. He seemed unable to make up his mind. He looked round and saw his fellow tigers lying down. He accepted that this wasn't the time for an attack. He settled himself as well and began to tell his story.

'We are Amur tigers,' he said. 'Our ancestors come from a land of silver birch forests and wide plains called Russia, far away in the East, so my mother told me. But none of us have ever been there. We were all born in cages. Myself, I was born in a place called Ireland and came here over the sea a few years ago.'

'But you aren't in a cage here,' said the fox.

'This is a cage, but a very big cage. Look hard.

There is a fence.'

Rubic looked, but it wasn't easy to see.

'In this place, it's different. They let the two-leggeds into our cage to see us. They don't let them stare at us from the outside through bars, squealing and shouting. The visitors are scared of us and so they are careful and quiet. They will be safe if they stay inside their tin boxes. They know this.

'Once, I have to say, in the cage where I was born, a two-legged put a hand through my fence. What did she expect? I bit it. I'm not a house cat. That was nearly the end of me, but it was decided it wasn't my fault and there aren't many of us Amurs left. Then, we were endangered. Eventually I was sent here. This place is good. We are respected.'

There was a purred agreement from the three girl tigers.

'We three are sisters, and we came here before he did,' said one. 'From a place called France. It was warmer there.'

'But it is good to have company now,' said another.

'But we want cubs,' said the third. 'And that isn't happening.'

There was a growl from the male tiger.

'I had cubs before. Lovely cubs.'

There was a long moment of silence.

Rubic could feel a sadness in the air. He understood. All creatures needed to know that young ones were to come.

One of the girl tigers gave a little growl and shook her huge head.

'But you,' she said, 'What are you doing here?'

But Rubic had another question the one most important to him at this moment.

'What do you eat,' he said. 'Do you kill things? You are felines after all.'

'Oh they bring us dead meat. We catch the odd rat if it annoys. We have eaten already today, that is why we didn't bother to chase you,' replied one of the sisters.

'If you are in a cage and get fed, doesn't that make you tame creatures? And yet you know the Words. Are you wild cats or domestic cats?' he went on. 'Are you free or are you tame?'

Turlough, the big male tiger, threw back his head and roared. Rubic saw the large pointed teeth in the open cavernous mouth.

'Pax, pax,' he said quickly. 'I am sorry. It used to be so easy. If you lived in a cage and they fed you, then you were a tame creature. Now it isn't always like that. It has got very complicated.'

The four tigers stared hard at Rubic. He edged backwards as he went on.

'And anyway felines have always been different. In my city they arranged our travel on the iron road and they understand the ways of the creature world. And yet the two-leggeds make them their pets.'

'We are not pussy cats,' said the second girl tiger, opening her mouth too, in a wide yawn.

'I do see, I do,' said Rubic as he looked again into another deep red throat and measured again the length of another set of long pointed incisor teeth.

'Alright then, so long as we understand each other,' said the third sister tiger. 'We do have plenty of time here. Tell us your story. But first,' she said and tossed a bit of meat towards him. Rubic retrieved it warily and gulped it down. He realised he now had to tell his whole story.

The story Rubic told to the Amur tigers is to be found in the book *The Running*. It is the tale of the escape of Rubic and his friends from the city. We won't retell it here but the tigers had never heard it before and listened and interrupted and asked questions.

When Rubic got to the bit about seeing the great moving water for the first time, the tiger sisters were curious.

'We remember, we remember,' said the biggest of them, named Svetti.

'Yes, yes,' chorused the other two. 'That great water that went up and down. We watched from our cages. We expected to get wet as it came rushing towards us, but there was a clear wall in between us and it and we just watched it crash and run down back into itself. It didn't get to us. We are felines and we do not like the wet.'

It was true that the tiger sisters had been shipped to England across the channel in a winter storm from their French zoo.

Rubic continued his story and was talking about his difficulties killing things for food and why he was returning to the city.

'If I lived in a place like this, they would bring dead meat and I could eat.'

'But,' said Turlough, 'you wouldn't last here. You are what the Keepers call Vermin and they would trap and kill you like the rats and nail your brush to a tree.'

'Yes,' said Soudari. 'That isn't the answer for you. Can't you dig up your food, like the hogs do?'

'What do you mean?' asked Rubic. 'I do dig up worms, but they are tiny and never enough.'

'No,' said the third sister, Shouri, 'There is something else. In the land where we were born called France there was something special under the ground. Men and dogs used to look for it.'

'What is it?' asked Rubic.

'I don't know,' replied the tiger, 'But it is rare and precious and good to eat. We used to listen to the Keepers in our birth land over the sea talking about becoming rich from digging up this thing.'

Turlough, the male tiger intervened.

'You should ask the hogs. They know. In the land of my birth they used to dig these things up and eat them. They know what is in the ground.'

There was the sound of a truck revving up in the background.

'You should go,' said Svetti. 'If they see you, they will hunt you.'

'But, 'said Soudari, 'it has been a pleasure to meet you and hear your story.'

'It was lovely to hear about the big wide moving water again,' said Shouri. 'We will have tales to pass on now.'

The sound of the approaching truck grew louder. Rubic stood.

'I thank you for your kindness,' he said,' and my breakfast. I wish you good speed, a good future and many cubs.' He ended his departure with the universal words of farewell: 'So Cheers Mate.'

Turlough replied for all the tigers.

'Good speed and a safe haven,' he said, again using the old words. 'And don't forget to go and see the hogs,' he added.

The approaching truck was near now, so Rubic ducked back into the bushes.

Rubic suddenly realised why he had felt such a sadness in the trees around him. He remembered his brother and cousins finding mates and building dens for the expected cubs. These tigers wanted follow-ons to tell their stories to.

He crept away and didn't look back.

'They are amazing felines, those tigers,' he thought. 'But they are so sad. It is too sad to be near them. I hope cubs come.'

He had learnt something though. Apparently there was some food in the ground you could dig up and eat, other than worms. If the two-leggeds valued this thing as food then it was worth checking out.

'Maybe it is like curry,' he thought. 'Must keep an ear open for it. Now, where next?'

5. An Elephant Friend

East was his way. He knew that. But it seemed a pity not to talk to some of the other strange creatures here. He thought of Butch, his brother, and knew he would never have agreed to leave this place without a little more exploring and a few more questions.

Ahead of him through the trees was another field with what looked like a big shed in it. In the front of it, near the fence looking over onto the road, there was yet another creature Rubic had never seen or heard of before. It was very large and a dark grey. It was far taller than the tigers and seemed to have a very long nose on a very big head.

Tentatively he approached.

'Pax,' he said.

'Ah, Fainites,' said the elephant. 'And who are you? Your kind are rare here.' She looked around. 'You'd better come inside in case the Keepers see you.'

Rubic slipped under the fence and followed the creature as she walked ponderously back into her house. Once inside she turned around and rather proudly waved her trunk at her surroundings.

'Do you like it?' she said. 'Just been completely refurbished. New walls, new floor, central heating. Do you like the colours? I think they chose rather well. I love the sand. It's my retirement flat. I am the only elephant here and they think I am worth it. Almost as good as in my circus days, it is.'

'Circus?' said Rubic, who knew the form and asked his question politely.

'Oh yes,' said Annie the elephant. 'I used to be a performer. I've heard them say I am the last circus elephant in the land. And I went everywhere. That's the one thing I miss, I don't get to do any travelling now and I don't get the audiences, or the children riding on me. They just drive past and peer at me from their tin boxes. It's a bit dull. No applause and no buns. Though I must say,' she paused, 'my arthritis has been a lot better since I stopped eating them.'

'So you were never a wild creature,' said Rubic. 'You've always lived with the two-leggeds?'

'I was a theatrical, ever since I can remember. It was a good life. Wonderful costumes. Red and gold. Processions, fire-eaters, acrobats all around me. Even a Houdah for the trapeze artists to ride in. In those days there was excitement, company, friends and a new place every week. Except in winter, when we all stayed in London for the season. Christmas was amazing. Full of glitter. Once there was a troupe of ten of us elephants in the ring and I was the baby at the end of the line and everyone clapped me.'

Rubic struggled a bit with all this.

'So you were the two-leggeds' pet?'

He found himself looking down another cavernous throat as Anne the elephant threw back her head and trumpeted. Rubic realised he had put his foot in it again and annoyed yet another species.

'Darling,' said the elephant, 'I was a performer not a pet.' She stamped her great feet. 'The two-leggeds and I, we worked together, to make a good show. We were a team. They do their best here, but it's not the same, no processions and I do miss the travelling.'

'My apologies,' said Rubic. 'I didn't intend to offend. I was asking to know. If you don't ask the stories aren't told.'

The elephant understood. She was a kindly soul who had worked all her life with the eccentrics of the circus world. She was not going to criticise another seeking knowledge.

'And you?' she said. 'Your story. Where are

you going?'

Rubic told his tale again, and answered her question at the end of his story.

'I'm going east,' he said, 'back to my city, where I will be able to find food without killing creatures and where more of the creatures with trees on their heads live. And I've been told about some special food buried in the ground that I have to ask the hogs about.'

'Well I don't know about that,' said Annie the elephant, 'But east. That is important. Especially at this time of year! You are in no rush?'

'Well no,' said Rubic. 'It's a journey, isn't it?'

'Then there is somewhere you should see. It is less than a day's journey from here, going east. It is a strange place. I saw it, years and years ago, when we set up the circus in a field nearby. Giant great arches of stone. Been there since ancient times. It is a temple to the sun.'

'Temple?' said Rubic.

'A place where ancient two-leggeds used to go and ask the sun to come back the next year. In winter on the shortest day, they'd invite the sun into their circle and have a festival. We, all of us, the whole circus were there one year, just before Christmas, me, fire eaters, stiltwalkers, lots of music, everyone. And the sun rose. It came into the circle, through the arch. It hit the biggest stone and everything was gold and shone and glittered. Everyone was happy. All that day and days afterwards, they came to the circus and put down their coins. We made a lot of money. The owners were happy too.'

Rubic had listened. He hadn't really understood everything the elephant had said, but he had come to understand that if he was not to be a settled fox with an earth and a mate then it was his job to see everything there was to see and keep it in his head, one day to be able to tell it all to someone else.

'East, you say?'

'Yes, it's an easy journey, the ground is flat and every path will lead you there.'

'Other creatures about?'

'I never saw any, but we were the circus. We were our own world. Anyway there were too many two-leggeds about for wild creatures to come out when we were there. You are the first that has come to talk to me for a long time.'

'Madam, ' said Rubic, 'It has been an honour to meet you.'

'You will come back? And tell me all your tales,' said Annie. Rubic realised she was lonely. She too was an 'only' like Pearl's friend the Harris hawk.

'Elephants live longer than other creatures,' said Anne. 'I am a good person to tell stories to.'

Rubic found himself promising to return, he couldn't help it.

'Until the Mela,' he said.

If an elephant could laugh, Annie laughed.

'I haven't heard that word in many years, since the old elephants from far away went to join the ancestors. They used to talk of "Mela". They said there were big processions and the sun was always hot.'

'My cousin said we foxes used to have a Mela on the Heath, in the big city. Meetings and parties where the follow-ons met up. That was the cousin who stole my beautiful love,' added Rubic before he could stop himself.

'Let me hear,' said Anne.

So Rubic told the whole story of the Polish fur fox. It can be found in the book The Running. Annie could hear bitterness and anger as Rubic told his tale.

'But he didn't steal her,' said the elephant. 'She chose him not you.'

'But I rescued her from the Zoo,' said Rubic. 'I loved her. She owed me.'

'She chose him. It only works if both choose. You must know that. It can't have been what was intended for you.'

Rubic had never meant to tell this old animal of his hurting heart, but now he had, it didn't seem to hurt so much.

'So what am I intended to do?' he asked.

'Who knows,' said the old elephant. 'You've

turned up here for a reason. I think you should go and ask the sun.'

That seemed to be that. Everything that needed to be said had been.

'Good speed and a safe haven,' was Annie's formal farewell.

'Cheers,' replied Rubic in the words of the Code.

As he trotted off leaving Annie behind, in her new house, he caught a faint trumpeting sound on the wind.

'Until the Mela,' he heard.

6.
ASK THE SUN

Rubic's head was full of thoughts and his heart a little lighter as he moved on. He thought about his little cousin Troy, who had been the first to remember the idea of the Mela. Such a puny fox he was, yet the one who had stolen his beloved's heart. She was beautiful, his lost, pink fox.

'But she did like to be boss,' he said to himself. 'She will look after Troy, but she'd have tried to boss me. It would never have worked.'

He mused as he trotted on. Annie was right. It hadn't been intended. And the vixens on the Moor? They had been lovely and kind, but that hadn't been intended either. He had reached a conclusion. He yelped aloud.

'I am a free fox, a wild fox and a travelling fox.'

'Ask the sun,' the elephant had said. Well he would.

While doing all this thinking, Rubic had been

trotting east. As he came out of a wooded gully he looked ahead and, some way distant, on the horizon, he could see the beginnings of what he thought all the fuss was about. He could see a stone arch. Trotting a few more yards he could see the standing stone circles of the monument the two-leggeds call Stonehenge.

'I must get up higher,' he said to himself. 'Then I can see all that is there.'

To the left of him there was rising ground, bare moorland. He ran straight up the hillside to its summit. Lying low on his belly, he turned to the South and saw what he was supposed to see and what travellers had been seeing for perhaps four thousand years.

On a flat plain, only a little below him, stood the circles of giant stones, some of them in arches, some of them lying flat. They were so clearly built and purposeful, that Rubic had no doubt that this was where he was aiming for. This was the Temple of the Sun.

As he watched from his hill he could see other activity. There were two-leggeds, lots of them, walking around the stones. They were traipsing round and round and then pausing to look up, but they were behind a rope barrier and didn't go in between the stones or under the giant arches. He looked again. In the grassy fields around the stones, he could see long-ears:

rabbits, lots and lots of them. They seemed to be moving towards the great stone circle.

Rubic had met rabbits in Devon. He liked them. They didn't kill. They ate grass and stayed healthy on it. They had never really existed in his big city except in cages fed by young two-leggeds. The occasional wild one that ventured too far into the city streets, soon found itself dead and eaten by cats or rats or dogs. As a feline acquaintance had said to him: 'Country bumpkins, rabbits. Not got the wits to survive in the city.'

They had survived very well on the Moor though.

'In their own place,' thought Rubic. 'That is what I am trying to find as well. My own place.' He looked down again. 'This grass must be good for them,' he thought. 'There are so many.'

He continued to watch the valley below him. He was in no hurry and the winter sun, though not warm, still shone.

The conversation with Annie the elephant had cleared his head and his heart of that dreadful, dragging, unrequited longing for his pink fox. He had a new sense of freedom.

As he lay there watching the scene below him, he realised that something odd was happening.

Those long-ears weren't moving of their own free will. Behind the great wave of rabbits, he could see small sleek fast creatures leaping and jumping and running from side to side, keeping the rabbits together. He watched more carefully. There was no doubt: the rabbits were being herded, like the sheep on the Moor. He watched a laggard rabbit being bitten on its leg by one of the small fierce creatures.

Rubic wasn't sure what he was watching, but he was sure he didn't like it. As he continued to watch, he heard a squeal not far from him. A rather large buck rabbit ran out in front of him and lay down.

'Do it now,' he said, 'I'll not be part of that. They've had my kits. My doe is in the Gathering.'

Rubic looked at him in astonishment.

'What, what?' he barked.

'Do it now. I'll not be an offering.'

'What do you mean?' said the puzzled fox.

'Kill me now,' said the rabbit lying back and exposing his white throat to Rubic.

'Not me, I don't kill other creatures.'

'You're a fox, aren't you? That is what you do. Well do me. Anything is better than that.'

Rubic, very startled, made the only response he could think of.

'Fainites, Pax,' he said, putting the two words of the Universal Creature Code together, unsure which applied in these circumstances.

'Rubbish,' said the rabbit. 'You're a fox. And

anyway, no one listens to the Words these days.'

'Yes, they do, said Rubic. 'In my world they do. Nothing would work otherwise. Creatures couldn't help each other. The two-leggeds would get us all.'

'We can deal with the two-leggeds,' said the rabbit. 'We are so many, and they are so slow. They don't give us much trouble.'

'Anyway, I'm not going to kill you. I don't. So what is going on?' said Rubic.

'It's them, the ones with sharp teeth,' replied the rabbit. 'They are our enemies. "One from every burrow," they said. "For the sacrifice." Then they say they will leave us alone for another season. But that isn't true any more. They just killed my kits, all eight of them.'

'This must be nonsense,' said Rubic.

The rabbit paused, for just a moment and then went on.

'Once, it was just the earth eggs they wanted. We would dig them and send a youngster with them to their den. Even their den used to be ours. It was the burrow of our Elder. Then the young ones stopped coming back. It used to be just one, but now it is always more and then more. And now they are taking any one of us any time, whenever they fancy. Not just at the full moon. They have become so many, through eating our meat, they just go on needing more and more ...'

Rubic had listened but had not understood.

'You are wild creatures,' he said, 'not tame rabbits.'

'It used to work,' said the rabbit. 'If just one of us from a different burrow each week, went to the Rex, with the earth eggs, those truffle things, then it used to be fine. They would protect the rest of us.'

'From what?' said Rubic. 'Out here, grass-eaters don't have many enemies.'

'From the gods, the sun. It is said in the Words.'

'No words I've ever heard,' said Rubic. 'What you are saying is, if one of you, from each burrow went week by week, to be killed and eaten by these little creatures they left the rest of you alone. Is that right?'

'Yes, but now we have the Mela and the Gathering. Tonight. And we all must go ...'

'Mela,' said Rubic. 'That word I do know, But that is all about a good time. It is when the follow-ons meet the aunts and uncles.'

'And make sacrifice to the sun,' added the rabbit.

'Not in my world,' said Rubic. 'I am sure that is wrong. Tell me, what began all this?'

The rabbit, whose name turned out to be Buckfast, began his story.

'There have been rabbits on this plain, by the big stones, since before the big stones were there. We have stories we tell the kits about the time when the stones came and how the rabbit forebears helped with their raising by burrowing and digging the holes. The two-leggeds pushed the stones into our holes and lifted them and they stood high above us all. That was a very, very long time ago, and not much changed for us since then until the little ones with teeth came, and that wasn't many generations ago.

There have always been a few little toothed ones, but we and they, we both kept to ourselves and things went on as they always had. Then the Rex came.'

'The Rex?' said Rubic.

'Yes. He was a big creature, as big as three of the little weasels, but of the same forebears. He knew about the two-leggeds. He had lived with them. He used to go hunting with a two-legged, but then he escaped.'

'That is good,' said Rubic. 'He is a free creature now.'

'He made himself the king of the sharp-toothed ones.'

'King?' said Rubic.

'Master,' said the rabbit. 'The Boss, Chief. He is the Rex. He organised them. Then he got them to start on us. He loves to eat these special round earth eggs that we can find in the roots of the oldest trees.'

'I think I've heard of those,' said Rubic. 'They are good. And you don't have to kill them.'

'He says,' went on Buckfast, 'that when he was with the two-leggeds he used to be given chicken eggs. They were nice, he said, but then when he was sent down the burrows after us, the long-ears, he found his first earth eggs. They really are different you know,' said the rabbit pausing for a moment. 'He said they smell special to him. The two-leggeds stopped him breeding and he is convinced the earth eggs will make him able to father kits again.'

For a moment Rubic was reminded of the tigers and the sadness their lack of follow-ons had brought.

'He said the little toothed ones had to make us dig for them, because we are the best diggers. He told them that they had to hunt for him and bring him meat because he was the king. He told them to say to us that if we dug for the earth eggs, the rest would be okay.

'It seemed a good idea at the time. But he eats a lot of meat as well as the earth eggs. Them, the little toothed ones, the stoats and weasels, soon got too lazy to hunt for him and themselves, so they took our kits to him. Then those little toothed ones decided we could feed them too and so it has gone on. More and more of us are eaten. And the little creatures have got more and more and bigger and bigger.

Buckfast just sat there with a defeated look on his face.

'It is a Gathering for the Mela tonight. Many many small toothed are said to be coming from far away for the winter festival. All we rabbits must be there. Look.' He gestured again towards the plain below. 'See, they have no choice. As the sun goes down it will enter the temple. There will be sacrifice and then the sun will come back and the days get longer again.'

The rabbit sat back on his haunches as he finished his story. He put his paws over his ears and pulled them down over his nose.

While this strange conversation between a scraggy thin fox and a rather large buck rabbit had been going on, a black and white bird had landed near them and was pecking idly at the grass.

'Pax,' it squawked, 'I've been listening.'

'Fainites,' responded Rubic, and then: 'I don't understand any of this. Do you?'

'Ah,' said the bird. 'That Rex. He's spent too much time with the two-leggeds. That can teach you bad ways. He learnt to hunt and kill but was never allowed to eat his kill. That teaches you things.'

'How do you know this,' said Rubic. 'And, by the way, what are you called?'

'I'm George,' said the Magpie. 'I know about their ways because my egg parents pushed me out of the nest and it was a two-legged mother who took me in and reared me and then set me free. Without her, I would not be. But that Rex, he was taught by different two-leggeds.'

'What do you mean?' said Rubic.

'For him, killing and eating got separated. He learnt to hunt, but not kill and eat. Now he enjoys the killing. I've watched him.'

Rubic had listened to the new friend, but he remained confused. If you were a free creature then that was that. You were free, you knew what to do surely?

Buckfast the rabbit, however, had also heard and listened to the magpie.

'You've seen him, the Rex?'

'I've watched from the trees. Only once. He is nearly as big as you,' said George looking at Rubic, who as we know, was not a big fox.

'He is a ferret,' the bird went on, 'and he has forgotten he is a creature. The Code says a creature may kill to eat but not kill to play.'

'It says that?' asked Rubic.

'Of course it does,' said the Magpie called George. 'And he has forgotten that. So have those stoats and weasels.'

Buckfast said again: 'You've watched him?'

'Yes. The stoats bring him the long-ears and then he rips their throats out himself and drinks the blood. He kills them for the pleasure. Then he makes those stoats skin the long-ears and give him the soft bits. He is huge and fat and just sits there. All he does is eat soft meat and earth eggs. The little toothed ones do what he says. I don't know why.'

'I've never actually seen him,' said Buckfast, looking even more miserable with his ears laid flat over his back. 'But everyone knows that if we don't do the sacrifice, the sun will cease and there will be darkness for ever and ever.'

'Come off it. Who says?' squawked George the magpie. 'The sun is for all creatures, not just rabbits you know.'

'But this is the Temple of the Sun. It all starts here. Everyone knows that.'

Rubic had at last collected his thoughts.

'I come from a long way away. And I have never heard of the Temple of the Sun nor have any of my tribe. I've seen the sun quiet and trapped in the trees. I've seen city lights at night which are as bright as the sun. But, at dawn, the sun always comes back. That is what the rainbow promises. That is what the Song says.'

The fox threw back his head and barked. And the Magpie joined in.

Rainbow, rainbow, rainbow too
The sun comes back for me and you.

The rabbit looked a little shamefaced.

'That's just a jumping song, for the kits,' he said.

'It so isn't,' said a shocked Rubic. 'It's the Song That's Never Sung. It's the Promise. It comes from the forebears.'

'What do you mean?' said the rabbit.

'I don't know,' replied Rubic. 'That's all I know. But it isn't just for rabbit follow-ons. That I do know. It's for all creatures. It's important.'

'I know that too,' said George. 'Even the two-leggeds think the rainbow is special. But that Rex has made sure the rabbits and those stoats and weasels have forgotten.'

'He can't do that,' said Rubic. 'That's not on. The Rainbow is a Promise. It holds the world together. Like the Words. Or things won't work. We have to know the world is here, until it is our time to join the ancestors.

'He must be stopped.'

7. The Battle

There was a silence. Then Rubic spoke again: 'I am going to stop him.'

'You and whose army?' said Buckfast the rabbit.

The fox was silent. It was the bird who replied.

'Perhaps yours. Look down there,' said the Magpie. 'Look, I tell you.'

They looked. Below them, the herding of the rabbits by the little carnivores was continuing.

'See. You see. Rabbits are so much bigger than stoats and weasels.'

Buckfast looked hard, then understood something of what George was saying.

'You are right,' he replied. 'We are many and bigger and many more than them.'

The creatures stared down again at the scene below them. The rabbits were now very thick on the ground, almost as close together as a flock of sheep going to market. It was clear to the observers that the numbers of toothed ones doing the herding were far, far fewer than the numbers of rabbits they were driving forward towards the stone circles.

It was getting towards dusk. The human tourist visitors were being ushered away by the guards. The creatures on the hill could hear motor engines spring to life and then their noise begin to fade into the distance as the vehicles carrying the tourists disappeared down the road.

'It has to be tonight, now,' doesn't it? said Rubic, 'Before the sun goes down.'

'Yes,' said Buckfast. 'If we wait longer, they will start the sacrifice and we won't be able to stop it. Those stoats and weasels will begin the kill.'

'Let's move then,' said Rubic.

With no plan except a certainty they must act, the three creatures began to edge towards the stone circles.

'Look, there's the Rex,' said George the magpie. 'He is coming out.'

The three watched. A small line of stoats came from a burrow entrance. They seemed to be the start of a procession. Following them was a very, very large ferret. He was at least four times the size of any one of the stoats he followed. He moved very slowly because he was so fat. As he progressed he paused and graciously nodded his head to the crowds around him. Behind him were weasels carrying what looked like round stones.

'See, the earth eggs. He takes them everywhere,' said Buckfast.

The listening creatures heard a sort of chittering sound rise from the crowd around the ferret.

'They are hailing him?' said a puzzled Rubic. 'But he is their enemy, their killer. You let him do this?' he said, looking at Buckfast.

'It didn't used to be like this,' said the rabbit.

'Creatures want a quiet life', said George. 'They want to believe in the world. They don't want to have to do anything.'

'It must stop. Will your grass-eaters rise and fight?' asked Rubic.

'Trouble is some of them have become meat-eaters,' said Buckfast. 'It started with the earth eggs. They give you a taste for things.'

'But will you stand?'

'I will stand,' said Buckfast. 'And some will stand with me.'

Meanwhile Rex the ferret and his retinue were reaching the inner stone circle, empty now of all but four-legged creatures.

Rubic, George and Buckfast, as they continued to make their way towards the crowds, could see how grotesquely huge and bloated the ferret actually was. Preceded by the smallest stoat, he progressed towards the big flat stone in the middle of the inner stone circle. He would pause every few steps, turning to allow the crowd of rabbits, stoats and weasels to view him. It wasn't praise he was seeking. It was awe he was trying to inspire in his audience.

At the base of the central flat stone, the littlest creatures stopped, faced each other, tucked their heads in and crouched down, making a step. Rex the ferret walked over their backs using them as a bridge and thus without a pause he stood in the middle of the stone circles, raised up on the flat stone. The stoats behind him followed and each placed a single earth egg beside him. There was a reasonable pile by the time all had put their offerings down.

The other creatures settled around the stones. There was an anticipatory hush. All eyes were on the flat stone. It was then that two of the bigger weasels pulled a young rabbit by its ears up onto the stone and held him there. The Rex came slowly over and looked at the captive and then at the crowd watching him. The chittering continued.

The Rex opened his mouth and turned his head to display his sharp teeth to the crowd. There was a gasp and the noise from the observers got louder.

Then with astonishing speed for such a lumbering animal, the ferret bent its head and bit off one of the rabbit's front paws. There was a high scream of pain from the rabbit.

The Rex raised his head with blood running down his pink fur, the paw in his mouth. He threw his head back and tossed the paw into the crowd.

There was a scrabble and a scramble to get the morsel tossed down to them.

Rubic, George and Buckfast moving onwards had watched the scene play out in front of them.

'No,' said Rubic. 'He can't do that.'

The three had reached the outermost stone circle.

But as Rubic spoke the Rex struck again and took the rabbit's other front paw. The scream wasn't so loud this time. The crowd again scrambled for their prize.

That's what he does,' said George. 'He'll finish with the throat.'

As the magpie spoke, the ferret reached out and held the white fur of the rabbit's throat in his teeth.

There was a hissing from the crowd. Rex listened, waited a moment, shook the now badly injured rabbit and then bit down hard with his teeth. A second later he held the white fur and bloody meat of the throat aloft. Blood spilled over the stone.

There was an intake of breath from the crowd and the chittering sound got louder.

'Then they'll bring another and another till the stone is covered in blood as the sun comes under the arch,' said George.

'No, no,' barked Rubic. 'This is wrong. It must stop now. Now. Come on. No more.' He raised his head and opened his mouth and from it came the strange fox yowl that all urban two-leggeds are both familiar with, and a little scared by.

The call sounded out across the plan. Rubic cried it out again. As he howled the fox charged through the outer circle scattering stoats and weasels and rabbits as he went. He continued to make as much noise as fiercely as he could.

George and Buckfast were momentarily taken by surprise, but within seconds followed Rubic. George took to the air and flew above the pair, cawing his loudest, sounding not unlike a two-legged's machine gun. Buckfast followed. Rabbits too can make a noise if they want to. Buckfast stood tall and thumped his back legs again and again.

Other rabbits in the crowd took up the signal and began to advance towards the centre of the inner circle.

Rubic leapt up onto the flat rock and faced the ferret. The two creatures were much the same size, but the fox, though scrawny was young. The Rex was fat and could hardly move. He saw the invader land in front of him and also saw that as he landed his paws dislodged the pile of earth eggs that the stoats and weasels had so carefully put by. The little round truffles scattered over the edge of the rock down into the crowd. It was the rabbits below who seized them.

This seemed to matter to Rex more than the attack. He scrabbled desperately for the last couple of the round fungi as they slid off the edge of the rock. He turned to face the fox.

'Those were mine, mine,' he snarled. 'I need them.'

Rubic didn't know what to say. He just growled back at the ferret. Then he opened his mouth wider and repeated his nightmarish fox yowl once more straight into the face of the creature.

Rex the ferret had managed to retrieve the last earth egg, He held it in his mouth, raised his head and stood up on his hind legs. He looked straight at the fox. He looked into the open jaws. He heard the awful cry in his ears. And something in his head burst. As Rubic watched, the light went out of his eyes, his head lolled sideways and he fell to the ground.

The moment the nearest stoats and weasels realised they were threatened, they leapt up onto the rock. They attacked the fox, but Buckfast and George were there and ready. As the first weasel tried to bite Rubic's leg, George used his hefty beak and speared the attacker through his eye. It fell dead. But it had many followers, who jumped up and grabbed any bits of Rubic's fur they could. He felt little teeth all over his body as stoats and weasels jumped onto his back, bit into his not-so-bushy tail, his ears and his flanks. He shook himself hard, but the little teeth hung on.

There was chaos on the flat rock.

George defended Rubic as best he could, hovering and diving and spearing with his beak. The foot-thumping call of Buckfast had worked. Rabbits answered and began to leap onto the rock in numbers, great numbers. They swarmed over the stoats and the weasels, almost literally smothering them.

It was a hard fight, but when those stoats and weasels nearest to him saw Rex their Ferret King was lying inert in the middle of the fight, they paused. They realised their Master was no longer there. They wavered. Those with teeth deeply embedded in Rubic's flesh let go.

The rabbits grabbed their moment and using their back legs literally kicked every stoat and weasel they could see off the rock. The panic spread to the crowd below and stoats and weasels there began to run. The rabbits followed, with George flying overhead cawing and croaking his rat-a-tat-tat call.

As the flight turned to a rout, the rays of the setting winter sun hit the western arch of the great stone circle. The sun sank that bit further and the golden light flooded under the lintel, through the arch. It hit the central stone as it had done at every solstice sunset for 4000 years. Rubic was bathed in orange and golden light. The creatures below looked up and saw him standing there, lit up, a great golden creature.

Rubic himself looked around and saw the body of the ferret.

'He has ceased to be,' he said. 'And maybe I have too,' he added, falling to his knees, battered and bleeding.

Two-legged human watchers later that night, at

the nearby inn, told a strange story. They spoke of a plague of stoats and weasels fleeing across the plain at the solstice sunset. Above them flew a giant black-and-white bird making a noise like a machine gun. Chasing the little carnivores were hoards and hoards of rabbits. Nobody at the inn believed them.

Many, many rabbits chased across the plain after the stoats and weasels, but some remained nearby. Several jumped up onto the rock. They found Rubic. He was in a terrible mess. His pelt was cut and bleeding. There were great slashes across his face and a half of one ear was missing.

A doe rabbit picked up one of the round earth eggs and, taking it in her mouth, went over to the bleeding fox. She pushed it at his mouth. To the very nearly dead Rubic it smelt amazing. He bit into it. It tasted amazing too. He finished it. Some strength ebbed back into him. He turned his head and began to look at himself. He started to lick the wounds he could reach.

The rabbit came back with another truffle and Rubic finished that too. Moments later, with a quark, the returning George landed on the stone.

'Well that's them on the run,' he said. 'They'll not be back for a while.' He looked at Rubic. 'I see you are still with us,' he said. 'What did you do to him,' he added pointing his beak at the dead ferret.

'I don't know,' said Rubic. 'He just fell over.'

'Scared him to death with that yowl of yours, I expect,' said the bird. 'Never heard anything like it before. Well, not that close anyway. Can you walk?'

'With another of those I might be able to,' said the fox as the doe rabbit came up with another truffle for him. By this time, Buckfast the rabbit had also returned and viewed the state Rubic was in.

'We need to get you off this rock, to a safe place,' he said. 'If you can walk you will mend.'

The fox polished off his third truffle and attempted to stand.

Some big rabbits came and stood beside him and supported him as he stumbled and slid off the rock platform. Slowly, slowly the odd procession of creatures made their way out of the stone circles.

'They are taking you to the old Elder's Burrow. It is where the Rex lived and the only one big enough for you,' said Buckfast.

It was a roomy burrow and held Rubic well. Once there, he collapsed and fell into a sleep from which neither George nor Buckfast could wake him.

8.
The Aftermath

Two days later Rubic did wake up and began to moan and cry. It was true, some of his wounds were healing, though he was never going to have a complete right ear again, but other wounds, on his flanks, where he had been so badly bitten, had swollen, become red and hot and infected. The fox had a fever.

Buckfast and several other rabbits had been tending to him. Even George, who being a bird, couldn't bear to enter the enclosed space of the burrow, stalked up and down outside the entrance. All the creature friends could see the fox was seriously ill.

Rubic too understood that he was near to 'ceasing to be' and as he thought about it he realised that he didn't want that. He suddenly knew his destiny. He had places to go and things to see. He definitely did not want to join the ancestors yet.

The feverish fox tossed about in the cramped quarters. He dreamt his feverish dreams. He remembered the past. He thought of his brother Blackberry and their journey, their Running, the longest there had ever been. He remembered his birth place in the Home of the Dead, back in his city. Somewhere in his head Rubic remembered the stories his grandmother Lucy had told the tribe, when he was a cub. It seemed so long ago now. In his dreams he saw his grandmother. She was telling the tribe the story of Blackberry being lost and found and mended. She always ended her tale with the words: 'and that is why we, the Cemetery Foxes, respect our Brother Badger, the Old One, who is our neighbour, and never take so much as a root from the store in his sett.'

Rubic realised he had one hope of a cure.

One of the older does was looking after the fox, She had brought him more earth eggs. He barked weakly at her.

'Fetch Buckfast, quickly.'

She was alarmed by the frantic urgency in the weak bark and did just that.

Buckfast arrived. Rubic was feverish but clear.

'Find an Old One. Tell him,' he said, 'tell him he is Brother Badger. He will know.'

Buckfast left the burrow and met George outside.

'He says we have to find an Old One and call

him Brother Badger. He is not getting better. His wounds are going bad.'

'Quark?' said George.

'He says if you say 'Brother Badger' to the Old One he will understand. Will you go? With your wings you'll be quicker.'

George, a magpie of few words, put his head on one side and blinked his sharp eyes at Buckfast.

'Quark,' he said. 'Quark,' and, spreading his wings, flew off.

It was almost a mile to the nearest woodland copse, on the edge of the fields. This was where the bird hoped to find a badger. He landed at the base of a slope, at a place where trees began, and looked around him. His sharp eyes scanned the trunks of the trees. He was hunting for a concealed hole, perhaps under a thick root. He poked among the fallen leaves with his beak.

It didn't take long to find what he was looking for. There was a hole, under a tree root, which looked as if it might be the entrance to a badger's sett. The bird was pleased to see his idea confirmed by the sight of old bedding and a pile of earth beside the hole. He stuck his head under the lintel made by the tree root.

'Pax,' he called and heard his cry echo down the badger tunnels of the sett.

There was no response.

'Pax,' he called again and again heard no

response.

A third time he called.

'Pax, Brother Badger, Pax.'

This time he heard a sort of heavy rustling and backed hurriedly away from the sett doorway.

Before long a snout appeared. The black nose was followed by a striped black and white face and finally by a heavy grey body. The badger emerged into daylight. He was growling and obviously not pleased.

'Arrrr! Who is calling me? And using the old words. Nobody, just nobody, disturbs me at this time of day.' The badger continued his growling and complaining as he lumbered out into the daylight. 'Who do you think you are? Weren't you ever taught? Waking an Old One is very rude.'

The badger paused and looked around for the creature who had called him with words he felt compelled to respond to, but could see nothing.

George, not a stupid bird, had retreated to the top of the bank above the sett. Badgers usually ate earthworms, but an angry badger had a fierce pair of jaws and big paws.

'Quark,' he said, 'and Pax again. It was me. I've been sent.'

'Grrrrr,' responded the badger. ' Fainites, I suppose. Now what is going on?'

Reassured, now The Words had been exchanged, George hopped down so the badger could see him.

'A bird! You're a bird. Since when does a bird come to name Brother Badger?'

'I was sent. Like I said. A sick friend. He said to find an Old One and call him "Brother Badger."'

'Hmmph, What creature and where?'

'He is a fox and it is over by the stone circles.'

'There's bad things been going on over there. I don't go over there any more,' said the badger.

'We had a battle,' said George. 'The stoats and weasels have gone. The rabbits and I, we chased them away.'

'Rabbits chasing stoats and weasels? Not sure I believe you. That'd be a turn-up for the book!' The badger almost sounded pleased. 'But that big one, the fat thing, called himself the Rex?'

'He has ceased to be.'

'Who killed him? Your fox?'

'No. No one killed him. My fox friend just howled in his face and he fell over. That was it.'

'And who told you about Brother Badger?'

My fox friend, he is Rubic. He was mauled by stoats and weasels. Some of his wounds have gone bad. He slept for two days and now he barks wildly and cannot lie still. His side is puffed up and red and pains him. He said to find an Old One and say "Brother Badger" to him. Like I said before. Quark!'

George was trying to be patient but couldn't see any point in repeating himself again and again.

'Alright, alright. But I haven't been called out for years and years.'

'Quark?' said George.

'Called out. Us Old Ones come if we are called. With the right words, of course. To mend creatures. It is in the Code. It is our task "Under the Sky". Even a bird should know that.'

However, having been thrown out of his nest by his parents and started his life in the care of two-leggeds, George knew little of the old words and old rules.

'Well I didn't know,' he said. 'Tell me.'

'I dare say there is a lot you don't know. You are still only a bird after all,' said the badger.

'But,' quarked the magpie.

'No buts,' said the badger, who seemed to have mellowed. Perhaps he was glad of the chance to exercise his skills. 'If I'm called I must come. Now where?'

George gave up.

'I fly,' he said. 'You follow.'

He flapped his wings and rose up into the sky. He chose his flight path beside the wood and along fences. He was an intelligent enough bird to realise that he needed to protect this badger as far as he could from the prying eyes of any two-legged observers. He had heard the talk of the guns which wanted to kill all the Old Ones.

As George approached the burrow where Rubic was, he could see Buckfast lying flat and low on the mound above the burrow watching for him. He landed beside the big buck rabbit.

'Quark. He's coming. He's following,' said the bird. 'I'd get everyone out. He is a badger after all. Big teeth.'

Buckfast disappeared back into the burrow and shortly after two small doe rabbits came hopping out and disappeared into the long grass. Buckfast reappeared.

'He is no better,' he said. He and George settled on the grass roof of the burrow to keep watch.

There was a sudden rustling and the badger appeared below them, right outside the burrow entrance.

'How did you do that?' said George. 'We were watching.'

'How do you think we've lived so long in this world,' replied the badger. 'We are the Old Ones, the oldest ones, long before any of you incomers. We come and go and are rarely seen.' He paused. Buckfast was about to greet him but he went on quickly, 'No time for stories now. Let's see. In here?'

Without another word, the badger disappeared

inside the burrow.

When asked later what went on, Rubic was unsure. He thought the badger had looked him up and down and then bitten into the throbbing sore on his side with his huge jaws. The fox had expected more pain but there had been immediate relief. He had been dazed but he was almost sure the badger then turned around and made water over all the wounds on his flank. The fox remembered the strong smell of urine.

When the badger emerged Buckfast and George were waiting.

'He'll do now,' said the badger. 'What are you feeding him?'

A rather timid doe approached bearing an earth egg. She pushed it at the badger.

'Those mostly,' said Buckfast. 'He can't eat grass and we don't kill things. That one is for you.'

'Don't mind if I do,' said the badger. 'A truffle treat is earned now and again.' He munched on the round fungus and everyone smelt the strange smell as it spread around them.

'But you do need to be careful of these. You do know that, don't you?'

'We used to collect them for the Rex,' said Buckfast. 'He needed them.'

'That is the point,' said the badger. 'He started to need them. No creature should do that, need them I mean. They are the rainbow's food. They are good for sickness and for the sun festivals, but they are precious, special and not everyday creature food.'

'So what then do we give him,' said George.

'Worms, lots and lots of worms and only one of these a day,' he said as the last of the earth egg disappeared down his throat.

'And only then till he is better. Then no more.'

'Well, I can get the worms,' said the ever-practical George, 'No problem!' He flew up and off to dig and hunt.

Buckfast had more questions.

'Old One, sir, we have forgotten much here,' he said. 'Rainbow's food, you said? And you called them truffles? Please tell us new things.'

As everyone knows, once a crisis is past there is nothing more a creature likes to do than share his story with others of another kind.

The badger looked around him and settled himself down. More and more rabbits crept up, anticipating a good tale.

'Us badgers,' he said. 'We go back to the beginning of things. We were here before the big ice came. Long before there were two-leggeds at all. Our ancestors have seen all the comings and goings.'

At this point there was a quark, and George landed in front of the burrow. He had both claws and his beak full of worms, which he promptly dropped.

The badger though disconcerted at being interrupted, looked rather pleased. Everyone is pleased when someone else takes their advice. The interruption was prolonged while Buckfast went into the burrow with some worms and shortly afterwards re-emerged.

'He's much better, he is coming to listen,' said the rabbit.

The fox's nose and front paws appeared at the burrow entrance. His head followed. Rubic began to poke at the wriggling pile in front of him.

'Not real creatures,' he said to himself and swallowed the first one.

As the interruptions subsided, the crowd of rabbits turned back towards the badger.

'You want me to go on?' he growled.

'Oh yes, indeed, Old One,' said Buckfast, 'There is so much we don't know.'

'Well,' said the badger, not a little flattered, 'As I was saying, we are very old. We remember the time before the lands were covered in ice and many very, very big creatures walked the land. Creatures the like of which you have never seen nor ever will see. Then the ice came and stayed all the year round and so the big creatures ceased to be. They couldn't find food.'

Rubic suddenly remembered why he had left the Moor. In a land covered with ice, few would eat.

'Us Old Ones,' the badger went on, 'we came south to warmer lands and we have watched as over the eons, the creatures have changed. We watched the birds appear,' he nodded at George, 'and then furry things,' he said, looking at the rabbits. 'Those wonderful big creatures never came back though,' he added wistfully.

'Anyway, time went on and the two-leggeds appeared and they learnt how to make fire and they built this place, put up these great stones.'

He paused again.

'With the help of the rabbits,' interjected Buckfast.

'I have heard that story too,' said the badger. If badgers could smile, he did so.

'I'm glad you remember the tales of your ancestors. The tales must be told, and the new happenings must be added to the old stories. All are important. They are there to help each creature know what to do when times get bad. And times always do.'

The rabbits fidgeted a little and looked a little pleased with themselves at being praised.'

'Us badgers, we were here when the two-leggeds who made the straight paths came. They were the ones that brought you, the long-eared, with them. You were tame creatures then. Those two-leggeds came from a warm place and to begin with none of you long-ears liked the cold. Many of you died.

'And now it is modern times. And we all know the rest of the story.

'It is because us badgers have been here so long

that we have become Brother Badger. If called with the right words, we will come and if we can, mend broken creatures.'

The badger finished his tale and looked around at the eager circle of attentive faces. None had listened to him like that for a very long time. He was a little ashamed.

'You have had troubles here. No creature should enslave others. You had become free creatures and should stay that way. I should have come sooner, I'm sorry.' He paused. 'But that's enough chat.'

With that he stood up on his four solid legs and lumbered over to the burrow entrance. He looked hard at the fox, whose front paws and shoulders were now visible as he ate the worms brought by George.

'Hmmph, you'll do. I'm off now. Us Old Ones, like I said, we are Brother Badger and will come if called. But don't do it unless you need us.' He growled fiercely at a tiny rabbit that had ventured rather near the big claws. It squealed and fled behind its substantial mother. He looked at George.

'Worms,' he said. 'Remember worms.'

With that, he turned around and, surprisingly quickly for such an ungainly creature, disappeared into the long grass.

9. Recovery

For Rubic the tide had turned. His wounds began to heal. George kept him well supplied with worms. Buckfast, having seen the effect of the truffles on Rex the ferret and the stoats and weasels, had understood exactly what the badger had meant about the earth eggs. However many times the fox asked for more, and he did, somehow the rabbit could only find one each day for him to eat.

Through the cold month of January, Rubic stayed mostly in and around the burrow. The snow came and then it went.

It was on a bright clear morning in March that a delegation of rabbits appeared at the burrow entrance. Buckfast, who had been living in the burrow with Rubic went out to meet them.

There were about ten rabbits of varying sizes, all does and each was carrying an earth egg.

'Well you can get rid of those for a start,' he said.

'That fox. He is a good creature,' said a large doe

rabbit. We want him to protect us and our kits. We've brought him the gifts.'

'No, not those. Never those.' Buckfast stamped both his hind feet together. 'Don't you remember? That's what made the Rex go mad. If you have too many, you can't stop. They are only for special times, for the sun and in sickness.'

'Who says?' The biggest doe was aggressive in her turn.

'The badger said. You heard him. And he was right. You cannot see the fox until you come back without the earth eggs.'

Buckfast was a large rabbit and stood firm in front of the burrow entrance. The delegation retreated a little distance and consulted. A small doe came to the front and spoke.

'When we come back, we can see him? We need protection.'

The delegation of does took Buckfast's silence as consent and they hopped off. Buckfast went back into the burrow. Rubic was awake.

'I heard all that. What was it about? What had they brought?'

'It was the females, the does,' said Buckfast. 'There will be kits soon and they are worried. They want you to protect them like the Rex did.'

Buckfast didn't answer the second part of Rubic's question.

'Come off it,' said the fox. 'That's not me.'

'I know that, but they don't,' replied the rabbit. 'They'll be back soon.'

Rubic was silent. He could see trouble on his horizon. There were crossroads ahead.

'We'd better get outside,' he finally said. 'And let's get George. He needs to be in on this.'

By the time the does returned, the three creatures were waiting. The battered but healing fox was lying at the entrance to the burrow. The young magpie was perched on a low branch nearby and the now really rather grand Buckfast simply sat tall in the grass.

This time there were even more female rabbits in the group. The smaller ones were carrying, with obvious distaste, mouthfuls of worms. These they dropped in front of Rubic and then rapidly set about nibbling nearby grass, quite determined to get rid of the taste of the worms as quickly as possible.

The largest doe spoke first.

'I am his wife,' she said gesturing at Buckfast, 'and this year I want my kits to survive. We need protection.'

'Why?' asked George. 'You are so many. You don't need just one to protect you.'

The magpie looked at Buckfast, who over the winter had become a very large buck rabbit indeed.

'I wouldn't argue with him,' he said.

The doe did look pleased, but she continued to

look at Rubic and went on.

'We want you to keep us and our kits safe. We've always had protection. The stories say that in times gone by no two-leggeds were allowed to kill us. They used to keep empty fields for us to have our warrens in.'

'And ...' said Rubic.

'Well,' said the doe, 'most of us were safe. We grew in numbers.'

'And ...' repeated Rubic.

'The two-leggeds would only take enough to be killed and eaten. They left most of us to become more,' said the doe, whose name was Myrtle.

'And ...' said Rubic once more.

'They may have used our pelts to keep themselves warm and put around their necks, ' Myrtle went on, 'But ...'

George, sitting on his branch, flicked his tail a few times, impatient of such excuses.

'Did you not hear what Brother Badger said? You have been free creatures for so long. Why do you want to go back to being slaves?'

'It is easier. And our kits will live,' said the doe.

'Well, some of them,' continued the magpie. 'You were farmed, you silly females.'

The doe was disconcerted. There was chittering among the other does behind her.

'But we will get things for you and everything. All you have to do is stop those small toothed ones coming back. You are big. You can't say no.'

'Well, that isn't what I do. It just isn't going to be me,' said Rubic.

'You can't say no,' chittered the rabbits.

'Well he has,' quarked George.

Rubic had more patience than the magpie. He understood what mothers will do for their offspring. He remembered his own mother risking her life and biting a two-legged, so her cubs could escape to start the Running. He still didn't know how she had fared in that chase. He looked at Myrtle again.

'Free or slaves?' he said.

'Living or gone to the ancestors,' replied Myrtle.

'Or a two-legged's coat collar,' added George.

'No,' said Buckfast, joining in the discussion for the first time. 'No. Didn't we learn something when the sun died? When the Rex went to join the ancestors. We were all together and we did things. We made things happen. We should be able to run our world and protect our own kits.'

'Are you going to do it?' said Myrtle.

'No,' replied Buckfast. 'We all are. Somehow.'

'You need a Plan,' said Rubic. 'We had a Plan for the Running and it worked.'

All the rabbits turned their heads to look at Rubic. Their ears were up and their faces questioning. Some were on their hind legs.

'And ...? So ...?' they seemed to say.

Rubic looked at them all and then he remembered.

'You need to start with a Talking, like my father had. Everyone is there. All have a say and a Plan happens.'

Buckfast understood. He got up on his hind legs.

'Tomorrow is the day the sun grows up. The time when day and night are the same. That is a good day.'

He looked fiercely at his wife.

'Myrtle, you and the other does go. Tell every burrow and every family to come to the stones tomorrow at sunset. We will not have a meeting, not a talking,' he paused. 'We will have a Rabbitting.'

Myrtle looked startled. She turned to the other does. There was more chittering. Then all the female rabbits turned to face Buckfast and chittered at him. The gist of their chitter could be summed like this:

'Well yes, alright, we'll do that, but don't you think you are the boss. This needs talking about, by all of us. Everyone will be there. We'll see to that.'

Rubic and George looked at each other.

'Well they seem to have got the idea,' said George.

'Wish you luck with that lot,' said Rubic to Buckfast. 'Rather you than me.'

'We'll manage,' said the new Leader Elect of the Stonehenge Warren. 'The spell is broken. I know

now. We have to do it ourselves. But it was you two who broke the spell.'

The fox and the magpie looked at each other. They too found they had made a decision.

'It's our time to go as well. Before all this starts,' said Rubic.

Buckfast was beginning to remind Rubic of another creature he'd met. He was remembering the Mareschalle of the Moor, the giant stag who was still leading his herd when Rubic began his return to the city.

Buckfast had become a leader and spoke as such. He had become the new Dom Buck of the colony. The rabbit went on:

'But we, here at the big stones will always remember the fox who gave his ear for us and the bird who speared our enemies. The tales will be told. Any fox or magpie who comes to our stones in need, can call on us for help.'

He stopped being the new Grand Dom Buckfast for a moment and said 'But what will you do?'

'Onwards,' quarked George.

Rubic's bark agreed.

10.
Onwards

'So we are going on together are we?' said Rubic.

'Quark,' said George. 'Why not? I'm used to different kinds of creatures. I don't like being alone.'

'Find yourself a mate, why don't you? A nest. Follow-ons.'

'No,' said the magpie. 'Birds are boring. I've just begun. It's a big sky. I want to see it. You know things.'

'Not much, I don't,' said Rubic. 'But I like birds. They see things I can't. There was a green and pink bird I knew once. Talked a lot to my brother. Helped us.' He paused, 'Ok, we'll give it a go.'

This newly made and curious friendship was to last.

The following day as evening came, the two creatures set off across the plain. They stopped on the hill where they had first met and looked back. Below them, in the distance they could see the stone circles.

Again they saw many, many rabbits making their way towards the central circle, but this time there were no herders behind with sharp teeth. Myrtle and the does had clearly done a good job. They could just make out Buckfast on the flat stone addressing his fellow warreners. It was clear a new era had begun in the Stonehenge Warren.

It is a puzzle how a fox and a magpie travel together, but these two managed it and made steady progress eastwards. Rubic had not forgotten the directions he had been given by his brother Butch and so they headed steadily towards the rising sun.

The two creatures settled down each evening to share their different experiences of the day's travelling. Rubic's view was from ground level with the smells and sights of the land, while George had looked down on the world from above.

Rubic was unaware of the work that Buckfast the rabbit had put in, saving the fox from himself in the matter of the truffles. But George knew something. He knew enough to know what was wrong when the second day after the pair left Salisbury Plain, Rubic became twitchy and irritable.

'You haven't had an earth egg for two days,' said the bird.

'So?' said Rubic.

'That's why you're so cross,'

'What are you talking about?'

'If you have too many, you'll go like that ferret

the Rex. They'll become the only thing you think about, but you miss them if you don't have any.'

'Shut up, stupid bird.'

George paused and stalked away from the fox to the other end of the clearing. He pecked idly at the undergrowth for a bit then he turned and walked back.

'It is time you listened and understood,' he said quietly without a single 'quark'.

Rubic, who wasn't feeling good, simply snarled at him and put his nose under his brush. George put his head on one side, looked at the miserable fox, and disappeared into the trees. He returned sometime later with claws and beak full of mushrooms. Finding them at all in March was an achievement, but the magpie had discovered a damp nook in the woods and harvested as many as he could carry. He dumped them in front of the fox.

'They'll not be the same,' he said, 'but try them.'

Rubic uncovered his nose and opened one eye. He saw the fungi and bit into one. There was a mushroomy smell, but not the all-pervading enchanting scent that comes from a truffle.

Rubic ate, and as he did so he felt some of the itching and longing and pulling inside him begin to ease off. He didn't feel the blissful peace brought by a bite of truffle, but he felt a bit better. He looked at the magpie.

'What's going on?' he asked.

'Told you,' said the magpie. 'When you were ill, you got to need them. Brother Badger said not to let you have too many, that's why that rabbit said he could never find more than one each day.'

'But it's just food.'

'It's more. The earth eggs are rainbow's food. Not for everyday. But these,' he poked at the yellow and cream coloured fungi, 'will keep you going. I'll show you where to look. They're good, you know.'

The magpie began to peck at the creamy heap, particularly aiming at the little black insects running around the white folds. Rubic joined him and the two creatures made a good meal.

It was several days, before Rubic, under George's guidance became skilled at nosing out mushrooms and toadstools. One evening Rubic's mushroom hunt produced something different.

He was poking about in the base of an old oak where he could smell and see his supper. He grabbed a mouthful of white toadstool and bit down. There was something hard in the middle. It hurt his tooth. He spat it out. There in front of him on the grass was a small gold ring.

The fox barked aloud in pain. There was a 'quark' and George landed beside him.

'Look,' said the fox.

'It's a two-legged's love ring,' said the magpie. 'A female must have lost it.'

Now everyone knows that magpies like shiny things and George was no exception. He picked up the wedding ring in his beak and strutted around carrying it. He tossed it into the air and watched it fall. It caught the light as it did so. Then the bird flew a few feet up and dropped it again. This time it tumbled over and over glittering till it reached the grass.

'The two-legged who reared me had one of these. It was her precious thing. Someone has lost this.'

'Well, two-leggeds! Idiots!' said Rubic.

George put his head on one side and looked at the fox.

'Like I said, a two-legged female reared me, when my winged mother pushed me out of the nest.'

Rubic's view was different.

'They chased us and tried to kill us. One of their machines broke my brother's leg. We had to have the Running to get away from them.'

'They live under the sky too you know,' said the bird.

'Don't care. They are the danger. They are the threat. Best kept away from. And they don't know the words.'

Neither creature was sure where this discussion was going when they were interrupted by human voices.

'It was somewhere here, I tell you, where we had the picnic,' said a female voice.

'Why on earth did you take it off?' responded a

second female voice.

'It got covered in honey and I licked my finger and meant to wipe the ring and put it back on, but then Geoff distracted me. We must find it. He will never forgive me. You just can't lose your wedding ring.'

'Well if you will go in for nooky in the woods ...'

'Don't be so smug. We've just got to find it.'

As soon as they heard the voices, the bird and the fox retreated deeper into the trees. It was Rubic who picked up the ring in his mouth and carried it with him. The two creatures settled down at a distance and watched.

The females were pulling at the undergrowth and turning over stones with no success. One of them finally sat down on a log and put her hands over her face. She began to cry. The other sat beside her and put an arm round her shoulders.

George had watched the females. Suddenly he picked up the ring which Rubic had put down. He held it in one claw and flew out into the clearing where the women sat. He landed in front of them, laid the ring down on a stone and then backed away. He quarked to attract their attention.

The second female looked up at the sound and saw the bird. She was about to wave her arms about to frighten it away when her eye was caught by a glitter from the plain grey stone slab in front of her.

She paused.

'Jane, look. Do look. That wasn't there just now.'

The first female raised her head. Her eyes were still wet with tears.

'Where ...?' she said

Then she too saw the little golden ring sitting by itself in the middle of the flat grey stone. In two strides she was there. She picked up the ring, laid it on her palm, looked at it, ran her finger round the golden circle and then slipped it back into its place on her finger. She held her hand up to the sun and the ring glittered again.

'Thank heavens. How? Didn't we see it?'

'Look,' said the friend, 'I think it's that bird.'

George had been hopping from one leg to another, watching the two. He cheeped gently at them rather than quarking. Any creature, even two-leggeds, could see he was a happy bird.

'They say magpies collect shiny things don't they?'

'Then he should have gone off with it. But he's brought it to us?'

'He can't have. He's just a bird.'

'He has. Just look at him.'

'Someone must have trained him to find things.'

'Maybe he was in a show or something? And he escaped.'

'We must give him something.'

'Got any of those sandwiches left?'

Bread crumbs with traces of ham were duly

crumbled and thrown in front of George. He hopped towards them and began to peck them up.

The ring wearer threw more crumbs to the bird. George bobbed and nodded in response.

'He is glad to see us you know,' she said. 'You can see he is used to people.'

'Maybe we should catch him? Maybe he is lost?'

The ring wearer held out her hand with more bread in it and George ventured up and took the morsel from her fingers. Then he hopped onto her hand and looked up into her face. Rather nervously she stroked him with her other hand.

'What do we do? Do we try and take him home with us?'

'Don't be ridiculous. He is a bird.'

The friend saw something.

'Look over there. He was just escaping from that.'

She gestured towards the trees. Rubic was to be seen crouched at the edge of the clearing. He had crept up to watch.

The two women looked at him in horror. One of them began to shout and wave her arms and Rubic startled, jumped up but George flapped his wings and flew over to his fox friend and landed beside him. The two women watched.

'They know each other.'

'They must be some sort of circus act, or they've escaped from a zoo or somewhere.'

'I know. They will have been trained. We have to reward them, something shiny. Then it will be fair. That bread wasn't enough.'

She burrowed in her handbag and came up with a key fob covered in paste stones. She held it up. It caught the sun and twinkled. She carefully laid it on the grey stone slab and backed away.

George put his head on one side and looked at her. He hopped to the stone, picked up the jewelled key fob in his beak and retreated back to Rubic's side. He dropped the fob on the grass and the fox picked it up.

Both creatures realised it was time to go before the two-leggeds had any more thoughts of capture.

They slipped back into the trees and disappeared. They could hear the conversation continue as they retreated.

'We had better tell the police or the RSPCA or something.'

'No let's not. They seem okay.'

'But someone will be looking for them.'

'Look, I've got my ring back. That's all that matters. Let's go home. We'll leave them be.'

'Okay, maybe you're right. We'll leave them be.'

Later that evening, the two creatures talked of their day.

'I just needed to know if she was my two-legged mother. I needed to look at her eyes. She wasn't though,' said George. He sounded a little sad.

'And what do we do with this then?' responded Rubic rather briskly, poking the pink jewelled key fob with his nose. Any sign of unhappiness made him nervous.

'It was our reward,' said the bird.

'What?' said Rubic.

'In exchange for us finding the ring.'

'But that was an accident.'

'Yes, but it was what they wanted so they rewarded us. That's how two-leggeds work.'

'So if we found another two-legged who wanted this pink thing then they would reward us too? What with?'

'What we asked for I suppose.'

This idea of exchange was new to Rubic, but he could see it had possibilities.

'So if we do things that others want they will give us stuff?'

'That's it. You've got it. That is how the two-legged world works. They call it shopping and working. That is what they all did, in the house nest I was grown in.'

Had Buckfast been there he might have had something to add, for after all, the rabbits had brought the earth eggs to the Rex and in exchange he gave them nothing but death and terror. Buckfast might also have said that the Rex's terror failed because the exchange wasn't fair. The rabbits felt cheated and finally fought back.

Such complicated thoughts were not in the minds of our two friends, however. Rubic was beginning to wonder if he'd found a purpose, a reason for being, even though he hadn't a mate and a den and cubs.

'Do we need to look for things that are lost?'

'Or things to be done,' said George.

That seemed enough thinking for one night but something had happened in Rubic's head. Maybe, he thought, there were other ways of living that didn't just involve eating and mates and follow-ons.

The pink jewel remained a problem. It wasn't useful, they couldn't eat it and it was difficult to carry. In the end they tucked it back into the tree root where they'd found the ring for which it was the reward.

11. New Beginnings

The next morning the creatures continued their journey east. As they circled round the outskirts of a busy-looking village they found a large long-haired, rather impressive tabby cat standing in their path. George quarked and flew up into a tree, but Rubic was well acquainted with felines.

'Pax,' he said. 'How goes the times?'

'Fainites,' replied the cat. 'I think I know who you are.'

Rubic was puzzled.

'The big stones, that ferret, the rabbits?'

'Well yes,' said the fox. 'That was us.'

'Would you come,' said the cat, 'and tell your story to us felines. I've been watching out for you. They said you'd come this way.'

At this point George, perched on a branch above both creatures' heads, gave a loud indignant *quark*.

'It's a feline. It kills birds.'

'The words,' said Rubic, 'you've forgotten the words. They make it safe.'

George remained suspicious.

'Who says so?'

'We do,' said the cat and the fox together.

'Were you never taught properly?' said the cat.

'No he wasn't,' said Rubic. 'He was reared by a two-legged mother. He still has things to learn.' He paused and recalling the conversation of yesterday added, 'but he knows things too.' Then remembering his manners he said to the cat, 'I am Rubic and this is my friend George, the magpie.'

The cat in her turn responded.

'I am Gabrielle and I'm the church cat. As I said I've heard of you and I am inviting you to our place to tell your story.'

'Why do you want us?' quarked a still insecure George.

'Tales must be told. The stories passed on. You should know that,' said the cat.

'That is the truth,' said Rubic. 'Stories must be passed on or they are lost for ever.'

'And anyway,' said the cat, 'it is the full moon tonight and we locals have our little monthly gathering and I'm supposed to provide the diversion.'

'And that's us?' said George.

'We do good food,' said the cat.

Rubic's ears picked up at the idea of different food. He was getting tired of vegetables and worms. George was doubtful.

'You sure we're not the food?'

Gabrielle was a little exasperated.

'Bird, the Words are important. No one breaks them. Without them, us creatures can't work together. I already know something of the fox journey, the Running. How would you have done that without us felines?'

'She is right,' said Rubic.

'Anyway,' said the cat. 'We meet in a place that you, a bird, will be fine with. We meet up there.'

She put her head back and looked up. Rubic followed her gaze. She was looking at the church tower.

'I am the church cat,' she said. 'That is my place. It is my job to keep mice out. We have a Gathering – we call it a Moonmeet – at the full moon on the roof of the tower.'

'We?'

'The local felines and, of course, the bats. They are our hosts. It is the belfry after all.'

'But bats are flying mice.' said George. 'Don't you eat them?'

'Actually they're not. That's the point. They fly so they don't make a mess in the church or eat the vestments, so the two-leggeds don't mind them, so neither do us felines.' She continued. 'My two-legged goes on about how they are protected anyway, but that it is better to have bats in the church belfry than his own. It is his little joke.'

George was quiet.

'Well, will you come?' insisted Gabrielle.

The two creatures looked at each other and nodded.

'Right then. See you at the foot of the tower at moon rise. Must go now. Arrangements to make, bats to talk to, supper to sort.'

With a brief meow of a goodbye, the large feline stalked busily off down the road into the village.

'Well, if we are being fed tonight,' said Rubic, 'I am going to lie up and sleep till then. Okay?'

'I'll have a fly around and check out that tower to be sure.'

'It will be fine I tell you,' said Rubic, but he could see that the magpie remained doubtful.

It was true. Nothing felt right to the magpie. He didn't feel he was a bird, he didn't feel any warmth towards the felines and the other creatures he'd met. He knew, but was sad to know that, though he had two legs, he wasn't and would never be a human two-legged.

The confused George set off to scout out the land. First he flew up to inspect the top of the church tower. He found a flat space well shielded from the wind by the crenulations and turrets and accessed from below by a small trap door set into a much larger one. George had seen something like this before. 'Those felines even have their own cat flap,' he thought, 'like in my two-legged mother's house.'

He could see this venue would make for a lovely party, under the full moon.

'And if those cats can really provide good food up here I'm all for it,' he added to himself.

He hopped up and perched on one of the stone parapets.

He could hear a sort of music from across the fields. The noise was actually coming from the sound system of a visiting circus. It reminded him of the noise in the house he had been reared in. There had been four young two-leggeds there and they each had to have a different kind of this musical noise, lots of it and loud and most of the time. It gave his heart another twinge.

He took to the air and flapped off to investigate.

'Damson's Steam Circus' was rather special. It was a travelling circus with animal acts, but it also ran many old fairground attractions that were powered by steam traction engines. It toured southern England during the early summer and then gradually made its way north as the weather warmed up. George flew down to investigate and found the circus folk were rehearsing for their afternoon performance. There was much noise around the site. Hurdy-gurdy organs were playing. Men were shouting, horses with feathers on their heads were traipsing back and forth in lines led by grooms.

There were other animal acts too. The previous

year the circus had added a bird act to their bill. It was rehearsing in the big top as George pushed his way under the flap. He began to watch.

The trainer had a trolley with her and on it were perched little blue and yellow birds. 'Budgerigars,' said George to himself, 'Nice birds. The old two-legged grandmother had one.'

As George watched, the budgies went through their routine urged on by their trainer. They jumped through little hoops and swung on tiny swings. Their trainer was a human girl in a costume which glittered with spangles that shimmered each time she turned. George watched her. She glimmered and shone as she twisted and turned and the spotlights bounced off her costume. George fell in love.

He continued to watch the budgies jumping on wheels and sliding down slides and pulling little carts. At one point a yellow budgie repeatedly pushed a toy car off the stand to the floor. It was clearly part of the act but George couldn't help himself. He stalked up to the car, took it in his claws and flying up, replaced it on the table. The budgie, who was well trained, pushed it off again and George replaced it again. The trainer watched astonished. She knew a clever bird when she saw one.

She grabbed the car before it went off the table again and put her hand in her pocket. She threw a few seeds to the magpie. George eagerly pecked them up. He looked at this human girl and then he did as he had done with the female two-legged in the wood. He hopped onto her hand and looked into her eyes. He knew she wasn't his mother, but he saw something there that twisted his heart. His eyes saw that she knew, she understood creatures.

The bird trainer who had once been billed as Zelda of the Flying Indians also found it difficult to relate to her own species. She had been born into the circus in her native Romania and for many years had ridden a motorbike on the wall of death. The previous year she had fallen off and now longer felt safe. But if you are born to the circus, you find a new act. Hers was the budgies. She liked the little birds. She and they got on well together.

She stared at the splendidly large black and white bird with the iridescent blue flashes on his wings who had crashed her act and was at this moment looking up into her eyes. She too fell in love. She stroked the bird's back and George bent his head so she could scratch his neck.

There was a cheeping from the table. The little birds were watching. Somehow, vows had been exchanged.

The moment broke. George flew down to the ground and left the big tent. He knew what he had to do. Zelda watched as the bird stalked away from her. She knew he would be back.

There had been another observer of this little scene. Curled up on the other side of the rehearsal ring was the circus cat. His name was Diabolo and he was a Manx cat, which for those who don't know, meant he had no tail and had never been intended to have a tail. He too travelled with the circus from place to place. He lived in the ringmaster's caravan. For many years he'd watched the humans and creatures interacting. He also watched the result of these co-operations. There was many a new circus act born of them.

As the years went by, Diabolo had become sadder and older. He missed the days when his big cousins, the lions and tigers had travelled with the circus. Things these days were rather tame, he thought, not even an elephant, just horses and those silly little birds.

Diabolo was not a fan of the Budgies, but understood well that everyone had to earn a living somehow. He watched the magpie fly away and also realised he'd be back.

George had his own idea of what he had to do. He took to the air and retraced the journey of the day before. He found the oak tree and poking around its roots, retrieved the glittering pink key fob. Carrying it carefully, he retraced his flight to where he knew Rubic was lying up waiting for moonrise.

He landed with a *quarrr* and dropped the pink

jewel beside the fox. Rubic, who had been asleep, woke. He looked at his friend. Something had changed. There was suppressed excitement in the bird's every move.

'Well?' he said, 'And why did you go and fetch that?'

The pink jewel lay between them.

'It's for a two-legged. I saw her today. She is all shiny and sparkling too.'

Rubic had no idea what was going on. When he'd gone to sleep he thought George was off on a brief reconnaissance. Now he was back and he could see the bird's feathers positively crackling with electricity.

He looked up at the sky and saw a yellow flush on the horizon. It was nearly moonrise. First things first, thought the fox.

'If we want supper, we'd better go and meet that cat,' he said. 'But something has happened to you. You need to tell the story.'

George, who wasn't quite sure how to explain what had happened to him, quarred his agreement.

12. The MoonMeet

The two creatures set off for the church and sure enough, at the base of the tower the lustrous tabby cat Gabrielle was waiting.

'See you up there,' said George and with a flap of his wings, took the easy route to the top.

Gabrielle took George by the more complex route. She led him round the tower to its main door. She pushed at a small door built into a big Gothic door covered with black iron nails. It gave and she crept through. With a wriggle and a twist Rubic followed and found himself looking at a curling stone staircase. He followed the cat up the dark narrow stairs, which seemed to get narrower, both in width and depth as he climbed.

He could see the cat's enormous fluffy tail in front of him. Suddenly she disappeared and in her place he could see a square of pale night sky. With another brief wriggle he found himself on the roof of the tower that George had inspected earlier. This time, however, it wasn't empty.

There was a circle of cats sitting on the flat roof and above them, mostly hanging upside down, from any useful ledge, turret or bit of masonry, were lots and lots of tiny bats. Rubic could see George already settled on the weathervane of the church, slightly higher than everyone else. The fox had never seen a gathering like it before. Looking around he remembered his manners. They had after all been invited to supper.

'Pax, Pax,' he said.

There was a chorus of answer, which could have been interpreted as 'Fainites,' but when voiced by bats and cats of various sizes and ages was really just noise.

Gabrielle saw herself as hostess. She began the introductions.

'Welcome all, to this our regular Moonmeet. Firstly, can I present Señor Mercylago, the senior bat of this Bat Cloud.'

He was a very small creature, though a large bat for his kind. Unusually he was standing the right way up. He nodded his head to the fox.

Rubic had never seen such a creature close up before. It really did look like a mouse with little furry ears, but with strange thin black wings. It didn't seem to be a bird as it had no feathers. The bat was no bigger than one of his paws. He stared rather. The bat's squeak could be heard by Rubic and was a repetition of the word 'Pax'.

Rubic realised what he'd done.

'Fainites,' he said. 'I've never even seen one of your kind before, so excuse me for staring.'

The bat stretched out both his wings and flapped them. As any creature would he took Rubic's remark as the accepted invitation to tell the tale of his species.

'We bats …' he began.

Gabrielle however wasn't going to have her agenda disrupted.

'Meow,' she said. 'There will be plenty of time for tales later. Let us finish the introductions. May I present our guests to this, the fifth Moonmeet of the year, Rubic of the Running and his companion, George.' She paused momentarily, listening for the polite chitter of welcome. She went on.

'Rubic, as some of us know, completed a great journey, but recently he and his companion have come from the Old Stones and have a new adventure to tell that has never been related before. Tonight I hope they will tell us their tales. Meanwhile let's give them a good Moonmeet welcome.'

There was more mewing and squeaking of agreement and greeting. Gabrielle ruthlessly continued with the introductions. She named several cats to the pair. They seemed to be creatures of importance locally. George and Rubic nodded politely.

'And finally,' said Gabrielle, 'can I introduce another friend, a regular visitor to these parts, Diabolo, the circus cat. His circus comes by once a year and whenever he can, he attends our Moonmeet and brings us the news.'

Diabolo stood up. All could see his tailless status. He was tabby-coloured with a white bib.

'I've seen you already tonight,' he said, looking at George. 'You've got stardust in your eyes, you have.'

George returned his stare. There was a puzzled silence from the rest of the audience.

'You were with the silly little birds and our Zelda.'

George said nothing. Rubic thought he'd better rescue his friend, though from what, he wasn't sure.

'Circus,' he said. 'I met a creature a little while ago who used to work in one of those. She was big and grey and had a long nose. She was missing it a lot. Annie was her name.'

'Annie, dear Annie the elephant,' said Diabolo. 'How was she? I miss her too. We both remember the great days, processions and really, really big cats.'

A slightly antagonistic hiss from his audience of domestic cats was heard and ignored by the circus cat.

'How is she getting on?'

Rubic passed on all Annie had said and told of her new house and added that she was a bit bored, 'but she gave me good advice,' he ended.

'She'd have done that,' said Diabolo. 'She was a

wise old one.'

Gabrielle had remained silent during this exchange, but now again reasserted herself.

'Friends of the Moonmeet, she said. It is time to eat. Let us give our guests a good meal.'

At her words, the cats turned around and from behind themselves produced a very mixed collection of foods. There were several opened packets of cat nibbles, some cheese, one or two very dead small corpses, an egg, two raw lamb chops and the debris from a number of dinner plates, obviously taken from bins. They spread all this out in the centre of the roof. Rubic was a little sad to see no half-empty silver containers.

The cats and the visitors began to eat what was in front of them. There followed a considerable squeaking from the bats, a cloud of whom rose up into the air. Small worms began to rain down on the pile of food.

'Our best, our best,' they squeaked.

'Those worms. They make a lovely dessert. If it wasn't for bats we wouldn't have chocolate you know,' said Gabrielle.

Rubic wasn't at all sure what chocolate was, nor why bats were responsible for it, but he was amazed that such tiny creatures had produced so many worms. He tried to show his appreciation. They tasted like no other worms he'd ever eaten.

'The vicar has a rather good wormery,' said

Gabrielle, 'and our flying friends can get access.'

George, meanwhile had hopped down from the weathervane and was poking at the pile of food. Diabolo, the circus cat sidled up to the magpie. He was a cat who never wasted time on unnecessary words.

'I did see you today, you know, and you want to come and join us, don't you?'

All a rather startled George could say was 'Quarr,' in acknowledgement.

'Hmmm,' said the cat. 'You haven't told the fox, have you?'

'Quarr,' said George again.

'Well,' said the cat. 'This is what I think you should do. Let us do the stories and we'll have you last. Then you must tell your tale.'

And so it was. Rubic was by now very skilled at telling the tale of the Running. He answered all the questions asked of him, mostly by the cats about their kin and his travels on the railway. He let George tell the story of the truffles, the battle with Rex the ferret and the visit of Brother Badger. George was about to continue when Rubic interrupted.

'Señor Mercylago,' he said, looking at the mass of bats hanging from the parapets of the church tower. He was trying to find the bat who had spoken before. A single creature rose into the air and squeaked a response to him.

Gabrielle meowed. 'The Chair recognises Señor

Mercylago.'

It was, after all, her meeting and her agenda. Rubic continued.

'Señor Mercylago, you began to tell your story. As I said, I have never seen your kind before. I would like to hear about you so I may pass it on to my tribe in the city. We don't have your sort there, I think.'

The tiny creature, even with his wings stretched out, was no more than five inches across and though all present on the roof could hear him, had there been two-leggeds present, they would have heard nothing, such are the limitations of the human ear.

'We bats,' he began, 'are old, old creatures. We too, like Brother Badger, have been here since the beginning. We, here, may be small but we know of relatives in warmer lands who are as big as yourself. There,' said the tiny creature firmly, 'there they are called flying foxes, not flying mice. And,' he added, 'we are very important in the scheme of things. We fly at night so we fertilise the flowers that only bloom at night. Without our kind the night flowers would have no seeds. The point of us is that when we are not there, the fruits do not happen. As our hostess says, that includes the cocoa flower, from which the humans make the chocolate they are so mad about.'

Gabrielle gave a knowledgeable meow at this

point. She had often listened to her vicar giving his bat talks to the youth club.

'There are many, many kinds of us under the sky,' continued Señor Mercylago. 'You say you've never seen us before. Well, you just have to look up. You have told us you are going back to the big city, where the four-leggeds have trees on their heads. Well, there, in that place there are many of us in those trees. I would add,' went on the bat, 'that we are unrelated to mice and rats or, come to that, foxes. We are, I am told, a nearer relation to the two-legged than to a mouse.'

Rubic, who had listened to all this with his head on his paws, sat up and nodded his head at the bat who had spoken.

'Thank you for telling your tale. We foxes of the city apologise for never seeing our bat friends and from now on, regard them as our cousins in the city as we do Brother Badger.'

There was a chittering of appreciation from the mass of tiny bats. Señor Mercylago rose again from the cloud.

'We graciously accept your paw of friendship and will make sure our relatives watch out for you,' he said. 'Now, if you will excuse us, we must eat, so we must fly.'

Gabrielle just got in her vote of thanks before the bats rose all together as a cloud and took off into the darkening sky.

It was George's turn to take the floor and he had learnt something by watching the others.

'Madame Chairman,' he said, nodding to Gabrielle, 'there is one more bit of my tale to tell.'

'Chair recognises George the Magpie,' said Gabrielle.

George stalked to the middle of the space on the roof, where the food pile had been.

'I was reared by a two-legged mother,' he said. 'My bird mother pushed me out of the nest. My two-legged mother was kind and careful. She didn't know what to feed me, but she looked in books and she found out. When my feathers came she and her own young ones took me out into the fields and taught me to fly. I have flown and lived, but a life with my own kind is not for me. I have tried, but I can't do it. I get on better with foxes and rabbits than with birds.'

He looked around him, unsure if his listeners understood.

'Today, as Diabolo says, I was at the Circus. I saw a two-legged there, all shining and sparkling. She was acting with little blue and yellow birds. I helped, I looked into her eyes. She wasn't my mother, but she understood me. I knew I wanted to be with her. That is my place.'

As he finished, Diabolo, the circus cat came up beside him and mewed. George understood. He hopped onto the cat's back, and from his new height looked around the circle of cats. Finally his gaze came to rest on Rubic.

'Quarrr?' he said.

'It's alright,' said the fox. 'I know. Everyone has to find their own place. I know that. Friends can only be close if their lives fit together. I couldn't stay on the Moor. You need to be near two-leggeds and I can't trust them.'

Diabolo the circus cat had the last word.

'We know the city, the place you are going to. The circus sets up there in the summer. We will find you and visit.'

George flapped his wings and rose up into the sky. He set off for his new home. He did, however, stop on the way and pick up the pink jewelled key fob. He carried it carefully in his claws and laid it at the feet of his new love. It was accepted and understood.

Somewhat startled at this unexpected end to her Moonmeet, Gabrielle managed nevertheless to make appropriate closing remarks of thanks and appreciation. Then she looked at Rubic. She was, after all, the vicarage cat and this fox was in her parish. The creature clearly needed help.

'I'll see you tomorrow,' she said. 'Us felines have had some ideas.'

13. To the City

She was as good as her word. Before dawn she was patting the sleeping fox's nose with her paw. Rubic was still asleep because after George had left he had been alone and he found he didn't like it. He couldn't settle. Eventually he went back to the wood and foraged. He sniffed and scented and finally found an oak tree that smelled right. He dug around the roots and found the truffle. He ate it and found some peace in a drugged sleep.

Gabrielle was a wise cat. She had seen most things before, including creatures over-fond of truffles. She understood the situation. Before waking the sleeping fox, she quietly removed the remains of the fungus, then she poked Rubic again with her paw. Rubic heard the meowing, but it took some time for him to wake up and understand what the cat was saying.

'That Diabolo,' said Gabrielle, 'He is a canny one.

Not reliable in the general run of things, but he will look after your friend, you know.'

Rubic grumped a reply.

'Not so much a friend. Not known him that long. Good riddance.'

Gabrielle chose to ignore this.

'Us felines have been considering,' she said. 'Why don't you get on the iron road to where you want to go?'

'But it's broken,' said Rubic. 'The feline by the sea told my brother.'

'Not up here, it's not,' said the cat. 'Only that bit by the sea. From a day's walk down the road, you can get a train to the station next to where the deer live. That is what those creatures with trees on their heads are called,' she added. It is very difficult for one who has taught many generations of kittens to miss out on any opportunity to inform. Rubic was in no mood to be told anything.

'I knew that,' he said and tried to go back to sleep.

'Brought you breakfast,' said the cat. She placed a piece of cooked bacon in front of the fox. The smell crept into Rubic's nose. He opened his eyes and sat up. He realised he was not behaving well.

He gulped down the bacon and felt his body welcome it.

'Meow?' said Gabrielle.

'Grrff,' said Rubic.

'Well,' said the cat, 'let's make a plan. You are

going to meet my son Charlie.'

So it was, some days later, very early on Sunday morning, Rubic found himself balanced on the little platform at the end of the brake van of a goods train, just as the sun began to rise. Beside him sat Charlie, one of Gabrielle's kittens from the previous year.

The goods train trundled along extremely slowly, clunking and jerking over every set of points. The brake van was the last in a very long line of trucks. The two creatures watched intently as the countryside went by. The young cat was nervous.

'We are to look for a place beside the line where the two-leggeds are growing food in little plots,' he said. 'I do hope we get this right. I've never done it before.'

Rubic couldn't help being sympathetic.

'Your mother isn't one to argue with, is she?'

'This is my first job. I have to move on from the vicarage. We are too many. She thinks the cat we are going to meet may have a placement for me. I want to be a church cat like her.'

'And the cat we are going to meet?'

'Well he has his own church, different brand, but the job is the same and his church is new.'

Rubic understood the idea of 'too many'. The foxes in his city had become 'too many' and then the hunters had come. That is why the Running happened. That was why he went to the country. Now he was coming back to his city because the country hadn't worked for him. He didn't really know why, because it had for his six companions, who all, now, had new lives.

'The point is,' the young cat went on, 'the church is not far from the railway, just beyond these allotments. We must watch for those vegetable plots, then two flags, one red and white and one black and white, and then we will see him, this church cat, and then we must leap.'

The young cat kept on repeating his instructions to himself afraid he would forget them. Sure enough, however, before too long, behind a wire fence beside the railway line the higgledy piggledy allotment plots appeared. Rubic saw the red and white, the flag of St George, rapidly followed by the black and white cross of Cornwall.

'Watch,' said Charlie, 'Carefully.'

Almost immediately, on a shed roof, they saw a cat who, as the train passed him, stood up, waved his tail, opened his mouth and yowled.

Rubic and Charlie jumped. It was actually quite easy, because the train was going so slowly. They found themselves up against a chain link fence. The black cat appeared on the other side.

'Follow,' he said.

He led them along the fence and then paused. They looked and could see the gap beneath it. They wriggled under. Even Rubic, who was larger than both cats, found it quite easy once he had a quick dig with his front paws.

They followed the black cat down little paths between the patches of broad beans where growing corn and sprouting brassica flourished. Gradually, the clunking clattering noise of the train faded into the distance. It became quiet.

The cat led them to a grassy spot behind a shed. There they found he had laid out food for them. It was the usual debris of city living: a half-eaten pie, a chicken carcass and a dead mouse. To Rubic, it looked delicious. He felt as if he was home.

The cat stood back.

'Welcome and eat,' he said, 'and Pax to you, Brother Fox.'

'Fainites,' replied Rubic.

'And welcome to you, young Charlie. Your mother speaks well of you.'

Charlie, who was a rather small tabby cat, tried to look modest.

The splendid and large sleek black cat went on. 'May I introduce myself? My name is Stefan and I am the church cat here. Apologies for asking you to travel by goods train. We can't be sure, these days, that the doors will open in these new trains. Two-leggeds have to press a button. They are not automatic as they used to be and they are so streamlined there is nowhere to hide. It is very hard for us felines of the iron road. They keep on changing things. We have to keep adapting.'

Rubic also introduced himself, but the black cat barely listened. He seemed intent on talking about himself.

'I have been offered a new position in the city in a much bigger church they call a Cathedral. I'm going to run our network there, and Charlie here is going to take my place in this church.

'And you, Rubic,' the cat tried the name out and then repeated it. 'Rubic. They tell me you have met the Big Cat? I am hoping to do so when I take up my new position.'

Rubic began to tell of his meeting, so long ago it seemed, with the big cat, Skimble Twelve, on Paddington Station, but this black cat wasn't really interested. He just carried on talking.

'I have to show you the way to the Big Park where the deer live. It is very near. Just one road to cross, then you are in the trees. Us felines aren't welcome there. If we are seen they call us feral and kidnap us. So I don't go up there. Neither will you, young Charlie.' Stefan looked at the young cat. 'You will always stay on this side of the road. We must be clear on that.' He looked at the fox. 'If you need to send news, you come to him. Is that clear? I have promised his mother to keep him safe.'

Rubic barked his assent. He was glad this cat listened to someone's voice other than his own. And Gabrielle's voice was forceful. On the journey, he had grown fond of Charlie, her son. The young cat was so desperate to do the right thing, but had no idea yet, of what that might be.

'Right, finished?' said Stefan looking down at the few crumbs of food the two creatures had left. 'Let's get going. We'll drop Charlie off at the church, then I'll take you on, okay?'

The small tabby cat and the pale red fox followed the large black cat once more. Before long, they found themselves on a wide green lawn surrounding a newish red-brick building with a little tower and a cross on top.

'Built in the 1950s,' said Stefan. 'Part of the post-war Catholic revival, after the coronation. We have a special set of prizewinning round stone pictures built into the wall. They have planted roses in front of them.'

Rubic had no idea what the cat was talking about, but Charlie tried to look interested. He realised he had better learn about his new home. He knew enough to know that the rules were going to be a little different from his mother's church, which had been sitting there for a thousand years not fifty, but felines made no distinction of allegiance. Churches were churches and church cats would serve anywhere they were sent regardless of denomination. The black cat was still talking.

'Charlie, you stay here and wait for me. I won't be long. Now you, Rubic, follow me.'

Rubic was not to be rushed. He looked at Charlie. He would say his goodbyes in his own time.

'Cheers Mate,' he said to the little tabby, 'and don't forget the Code. The Words. They are important.' He paused. 'Your mother was good to me. I will come and see you when I can.'

Charlie gave a nervous mew. He was very aware that his future lay in the black cat's paws and didn't want to offend him.

Stefan watched approvingly and then set off.

'Follow,' he said and Rubic did.

They didn't go far. Once on the pavement outside the church grounds, the cat turned left and walked a very short distance. He stopped on some bumpy paving stones, beside the road.

'This is a crossing,' he said to the fox, 'to avoid those tin boxes with wheels. They go very fast here.'

Rubic was affronted.

'I was begun in the city,' he said. 'I know about crossings.'

'Well,' said the cat, ignoring Rubic, 'When I say go, you go. Up that little road, then you will see a way through to trees. Keep south and you will meet the deer.' He paused, then he too said his formal farewell. 'Cheers mate. Good speed and a safe haven.'

'Until the Mela,' said Rubic, unsure what he should have said and equally sure he was glad to say goodbye to this particular feline.

The black cat watched the road.

'Go,' he said.

14. Big Park

Rubic did as he was told. He ran swiftly across the white stripes on the road, up the little lane facing him, turned right and found himself in a wood. He followed a path through tall trees.

In the dim dawn light, he saw a huge grey spiky thing towering over him. For a moment he was alarmed, but then his nose told him it was dead and a tree. He looked again. He had never seen anything like it before. It seemed to be a sprouting of many dead branches into a spiky whole of dead white wood. It was at least eight feet high. Rubic knew immediately who he wanted to tell about it.

'Butch would love to see this,' he thought. 'It's a Wyche tree.'

A moment later his nose caught another familiar smell. It was the smell of dead-and-buried two-leggeds. On the other side of the path, through the trees he could see gravestones. He whimpered with pleasure. He had been born in a cemetery and those rows of grey stones were the scent of home to him.

It wasn't difficult to gain entry. He four-padded his way onto grassy avenues created by placing the rows of gravestones back to back. Looking around, he couldn't find the stone he was used to seeing, the one of the big man, where his tribe, in his own birth cemetery, had held their Talkings. The biggest stone he could see around here was that of a bright green female with great wings on her back and with no nice shelter beneath her at all.

Rubic was tired. It had been a long journey. New friends had come and gone. He hadn't seen any of his own kind for weeks. At least, thanks to the church cat, he'd had breakfast. He knew this place would come alive soon, when the two-leggeds woke up. He knew he had to hide and hadn't the heart in him to search further for a safer place.

He looked around again and saw a copse of trees in the middle of a grassy lawn. He investigated and found a sanctuary. It was overgrown with weeds, but there was a stone bench and the whole was surrounded by raggedy yew bushes and trees.

He crept into the copse and under the stone bench, put his paws over his nose and slept.

He slept all day. It was dusk when he woke. The cemetery was quiet. There were no two-leggeds. Everyone had gone home. The gates were locked. Rubic opened one eye and then the other. As consciousness returned, a great weight seemed to descend on him from somewhere.

'Well, I'm here, so what?' he thought.

He realised he had been so consumed with the idea of the journey, he hadn't thought about what to do when he arrived. He wanted to meet the deer, but what was he going to say?

He was deflated. As he woke and stretched he began to feel another twitch, almost a pain in his insides. He wanted, 'No,' he thought, 'I need an earth egg.' That would make him feel better, he knew. He remembered the advice of the badger and even though he had said nothing, he had been aware of the rationing of his truffle supply by George. He knew too that Gabrielle had carefully tidied away his leftovers. He knew they were acting for his own good. But they weren't here now, were they?

Rubic was alone and lonely. He remembered the last time he had felt like this. It had been bad. And it had been before he had ever even seen a truffle. It had been when he was on the road. At that moment, joining the ancestors seemed a good idea. And then he had tried to race the tin boxes. And then he had felt better.

He needed to move. He knew that. But what to do? Then he remembered the Wyche tree he had seen early that morning. He would go back and look at it. Young Pearl thought some things were important. She thought her green glass ball was one of them. That strange naked dead tree standing high above the path seemed so too.

It wasn't too far away. He got up, trotted across the grass and through the fence. He was back in the little wood with the high tall trees that seemed to go right up to the clouds. It reminded him of one reason why the foxes left the city in the beginning.

'The sun would be trapped in those branches,' he thought. 'That's what Blackberry used to say. He was right. I don't like it here.'

He came to the base of the strange spiky dead tree and walked around it.

The keepers of the common would have been able to tell him how it had come about. It was a coppiced elder that had been poisoned and died. Before the keepers had time to clear it away, the dead tree it had become a happening, a something, a Wyche tree. Children liked it. They put flowers and fir cones around it. Their parents told them stories about it. There had been a public protest and now the dead tree would be allowed to stay till it fell to pieces of its own accord.

The keepers came reluctantly from time to time and cleared up the more bizarre offerings from both two-leggeds and indigenous creatures. As far as they were concerned it was dead wood and should be got rid of.

Not only two-leggeds loved the tree. Birds perched there to survey the surrounding area in safety. Creatures found it a safe meeting place.

Peculiar natural places do attract homage. Big oaks and yew trees have always done so, as have tall rocks and an unexpected hill in the middle of a plain. There is a tendency to create shrines amongst both creatures and the two-legged. It is a way to salute nature. In a city, the opportunities are more limited, so here, on this small piece of common land, a dead coppiced elder had become a Wyche tree, the focus of the need for all to have sacred places.

Rubic knew none of this. He just knew he was drawn to the strange grey and white spiky thing. He walked around the dead tree a second time. It was all of nine foot around. As he completed his second circle, wondering what he was supposed to do next, there was a squawk from above him.

He looked up. There was a bright green bird with an equally bright pink beak looking down at him. Rubic barked excitedly.

'Pax, Pax, are you Jendrix? I knew him.'

'Fainites,' said the bird. 'No, I'm not, but he is a relation and I've heard of you.'

'And I of your kind,' said Rubic. 'I know your stories. Without Jendrix to help, my brother could never have made a map in his head and we would never have been able to do the Running.'

The ring-necked parakeet was flattered as is any creature who meets another and discovers his story is already known. The bird preened himself and raised a claw to scratch his head.

'And what are you doing walking round the Wyche Tree?'

'Just walking round it – to see it.'

'Well I should be careful if I was you. Walk round it three times and you are asking.'

'Asking what?'

'Whatever you choose.'

'Will it happen?'

'Who knows, but there is always a price.'

'I don't understand.'

'Neither do we really. But I'd stay where you are for now, if I was you. If you go round again, who knows? Anyway, tell me what are you doing here.'

'Well,' said Rubic, ' I had to come back. I was hungry down there.'

'City folk are always city folk,' said the parakeet.

'And,' said Rubic, 'I met the creatures with trees on their heads, the deer and they told me they had cousins in the city.'

'True, said the parakeet, 'but what do you want with them? You are a fox.'

Rubic was stumped. How could he explain?

'I ran with them,' he said. 'We all did. They were free.'

'Hmm,' said the parakeet. 'Well it isn't as easy as that up here.'

'But where are they?' said Rubic. 'I can't see them. They said they were here.'

'Not far,' said the bird. 'But listen. This is a city.

Freedom is complicated in a city.'

Rubic had no intention of listening.

'Where are they then?' he said.

'Not far,' said the bird again, 'but listen, really listen. At least you must offer to the Wyche tree.'

Rubic barked a question mark.

'For luck or something,' said the bird, 'Perhaps to stop bad things happening. I don't know. The two-leggeds do it and now so do we. You must put a pine cone or something there or I won't be responsible.'

Rubic had no desire to cause offence and he still hadn't been told where the deer were, so he did what he was told. He went a little way down the path and found a nice fat pine cone and with his teeth placed it at the base of the spiky Wyche tree. The parakeet looked relieved.

'No point in looking for trouble,' he said. 'Now, your way. It is easy. Follow this path until you meet an iron gate and a wall. Go through the gate and you will find the deer. There are many of my family up there. If you need help, just ask for me, Ned of Aus.'

Rubic couldn't resist it. He had to ask.

'Of Aus?' he said.

'Ah,' replied the parakeet. 'There are many of my cousins in a place very far away, but we hear from them occasionally and we keep the names going. I am called after a famous two-legged from there:

Ned Kelly. He was a wild one, they say.'

Rubic did manage to resist the urge to ask how this parakeet got messages from a place so far away.

He turned his mind to his own affairs and trotted up the path between the tall trees. He still didn't feel right. He didn't like this path, or the trees. The wood was dark. It pressed down on him. It didn't feel free. He could barely see the sky.

As he trotted along, he began to wonder: had this whole journey been a mistake? What was he doing here? Had he simply run away? Perhaps he should have stayed put, learnt to eat small creatures and stopped making a fuss? Was he just a coward?

Moments later, the promised brick wall appeared in front of him with the tall iron gate set into it. For a skinny fox like Rubic, it was a brief wriggle and he was through the railings.

He looked around. The trees were gone. There was an open sky. It was light. The land was open. It was like the Moor he had left behind. It was okay. This was land he liked. He ran out onto the cropped grass, jumped into the air, chased a passing insect and generally skittered about. He lay on his back and rubbed himself against the short turf. The smell was good. His doubts vanished as quickly as they had come.

He set off up a slight incline towards a bare horizon. He could see that this was land on which deer could live.

'Now to find them,' he thought.

15. The Dream Come True?

The first creature he saw wasn't a deer, it was a brown rabbit. Rubic ignored it. He wasn't prepared to get into conversation with any other species until he had seen the creatures he had come so far to see. He pressed on up the hill. Then, to his left, he saw them.

There was a male with antlers on his head and several does and some fawns. They were lying on the grass in the shade of an oak tree. The early sun shone through its branches. The dappled light broke up the deer silhouettes and made them almost invisible. Rubic went over to them.

'Pax, pax,' he barked. 'I have come a long way to talk to you.'

The deer raised his head. He barked some words back. Rubic could just distinguish something that sounded like 'Fainites', but the rest he couldn't understand. There was a small voice at his side.

'Don't worry. They don't talk like us. It takes practice to know what they are saying.'

Rubic looked down and saw a brown rabbit very like the one he had just ignored. The creature continued.

'I've been following you.'

Rubic remembered what the Mareschalle of the Moor had said to him.

'They're the little Frenchies, aren't they?'

'Yup,' said the rabbit. 'With practice you get to know what they are talking about. They never change the way they say their words though. We just have to learn to understand them. And you'd better not call him little. It'll offend.'

The little buck deer meanwhile continued to stare at Rubic. Then he bent his head and continued to graze.

'Look,' said the rabbit, 'Let's go. He heard you. He'll never talk to you now.'

'But ...' said a confused Rubic.

'Listen, I'll take you to meet the Mareschalle, the head of the King's deer, the red deer. Just don't put your paw in it again, okay?'

The rabbit set off further up the hill. Rubic followed. He was upset. He'd never offended another creature before. He'd used the words and they hadn't worked. Most species were eager to talk. It was confusing. The rabbit stopped at the brow of the hill.

'Look,' he said. 'There he is. Now go down there and say your piece. Don't rush it. He's not got the sharpest points, that one.'

Rubic looked confused. The rabbit explained.

'It's what we say if one of the King's deer isn't as clever as maybe he should be. Suggests his antlers aren't up to it. He is supposed to be their leader, after all.'

Rubic turned to thank the rabbit.

'No prob. You'll see me again. I've heard you have a story to tell about how my kind helped you save the day. News gets around, you know. Off you go.'

Rubic looked down the hill. He could see the red deer stag standing there with his head thrown back, watching his hinds and their calves. This stag had the biggest tree branches on his head that Rubic had seen on any stag, even on the moor. It was spring, so they were soft and brown and furry, unlike the hard dry bony things of the previous autumn that Rubic had got used to seeing lying about on the moor.

He trotted up towards the stag, but wary of the great antlers, paused at a distance.

'Pax, Pax,' he barked.

There was a hind, standing beside the stag. She saw and heard him first. She gave the stag a quick nip on the neck with her muzzle to attract his attention. He turned around, saw Rubic and lowered his antlers. He stamped his foot preparing to charge. The hind snickered something to him. He stopped in his tracks.

Rubic called again. 'Pax, pax.'

'Er, fainites,' came the hesitant answer from the stag.

Rubic approached the tall creature with respect.

'I have come a long way to see you,' he said. 'I ran with your cousins on the Moor and I bring greetings from them. They told me many tales of you and yours.'

'Uhh. What have they been saying? I can't help it you know.'

Rubic didn't understand this and repeated his greeting. He then went on to repeat what the Mareschalle of the Moor had said to him.

'I have been told that the two-leggeds walk among you and you aren't hunted, but you are free.'

'True, true,' said the stag. 'They come and look at us and drive by in their tin boxes, ever so slowly.'

His hind intervened.

'But there is the wall. We can't get out. It goes all the way round and beyond is the city. '

'That means you aren't free, if you can't go anywhere you want.' said Rubic. 'When I lived in this city before, I could go anywhere, but that meant I was hunted.'

'This word "free", who told you about it?' asked the stag.

'It is our word. Us, the foxes, we are free. We are wild.'

'Well, it isn't our word,' said the big stag,' giving Rubic the same look that the Mareschalle on the Moor had. The hind beside him was shaking her head, but said nothing. Rubic thought he had better change the subject. He went for a neutral topic, the legends.

'They told me as well, that you were special and were Guardians of the grave of a dead two-legged king.'

His attempt at peace-making wasn't a success. The stag raised his head. He looked fiercely at the fox.

'I knew they knew. It wasn't my fault. I was never told. But it wasn't my fault. It wasn't my fault.'

The stag stamped his feet, bent his huge head and shook his great antlers at Rubic.

'They came. They took my uncle. He was the one with the knowledge. They took him. And I don't know, I don't know, I just don't know. I was never told, I say.' He threw back his head and roared. 'Oh woe, woe is me! I have lost the secret of the tribe.'

The fox wasn't frightened. He'd seen much in his travels. He was a wise fox now. He knew confusion and misery when he saw it. The stag opened his mouth, roared again.

'Just go away, go away, go away. Leave me alone.'

The Grand Mareschalle of the city deer turned his back on the fox and simply galloped off.

His hind remained behind. She looked sad.

Rubic may not have been frightened by the huge animal, but he was shocked. He lay down. He had come all this way to fulfil his dream: his dream of running with the city deer. And now it seems it was a fantasy. It wasn't going to happen. The deer, they didn't run. They were behind a wall and their Grand Mareschalle didn't seem the wise leader the fox had expected.

The hind spoke.

'It's not his fault. It really isn't. I am his Lady, the oldest hind. I will tell you our story.'

She lay down near Rubic and began to speak. The fox raised his head and looked at her. She was beautiful. He didn't think he's seen such beauty since he fell in love with his beautiful pink Polish fox Piana. He listened.

'I know the words you talk of. We, the hinds, we remember these things. He has forgotten or never known very much. He is so unhappy now. He was never intended, you see. His brother was the eldest and a clever leader. He was too clever. The two-leggeds who watch us realised that. He could open gates and get at the good young trees. He knew all the byways here. He was the intended and so had all the secrets given him by his father. He wasn't as big as his brother, nor did he have as many points on his head, but he was clever and they noticed, so when the cull came they took him and left his brother.

'Those two-leggeds, they like us to be handsome

and stupid. That's the sort of deer they like to see. We, the hinds, try to look just that and we keep our heads down.'

There was a lot in this Rubic didn't understand, but the one thing he did know was that he would do anything to please this beautiful creature. He was falling in love again. He tried to keep the conversation going.

'Cull?' he said. 'What is that?'

'In spring they take young stags, in autumn they take hinds. They take our best and our cleverest. They took my beautiful son. And last year, like I said, they took our Grand Mareschalle as well, because he was too clever for them.'

'Took them? Where?'

'Killed them. They send our meat to be sold.'

'You mean they cease to be?' Rubic wasn't sure he believed his ears. 'And you all let it happen?'

'What can we do?'

'Well ...'

'I know about your Grand Running. The Frenchie doe, La Reine, she told me. But we can't run. We have a wall and anyway we are deer and we are big. We can't slide into hedges and hide in corners like foxes and rats.'

'But ...'

'We survive. We are still here and have been for many a hundred year.'

There was pride in her response.

'You are content?'

'Well, we would manage if our Mareschalle would behave right. At the moment he is a little mad, I think. He is charging around and roaring and stuff.'

'Why? Is he ill?'

'It's the worry about the dead king and where he is buried. That's the secret he should know and hasn't been told. He thinks he has lost the heritage of our tribe, our reason for being. The Secret. If he goes on like this they will take him too for the cull. He is just supposed to stand there and look grand and splendid. If he doesn't they will take him. But he is so unhappy because he has lost the Secret.'

Rubic thought. He was silent for a bit. In his head he had thoughts. He realised, these creatures, these magnificent deer, weren't free at all, they were farmed. He looked at the so sad and intelligent soft creature in front of him. He realised he adored this Lady but now being an older and wiser fox he didn't voice his thoughts.

'Can I help?' he said. 'We saved the Mareschalle of the Moor from the gun. Can I help here?' He thought again, of the golden ring and the pink jewel and a conversation with George the magpie. 'I am good at finding things,' he said.

The hind lifted her head and Rubic saw a gleam of hope in her sad eyes. His heart told him he had to serve her.

'Could you find the King's Grave for him? So he

knows. So he can be proud and stop being mad? He is a great big stupid stag, but he is my stag and I want him happy.'

'I could try,' said Rubic the fox, looking deeply into the hind's eyes. He would serve her, he thought, come what may.

'I will talk to him,' said the hind. 'Come back tonight when the gates are shut.'

The hind stood up on her long thin legs, looked around.

'My name is Stella,' she said and set off to find her stag.

Rubic lay on the grass and thought.

'I heard all that,' said a voice. 'She is quite right. His days are numbered unless he calms down. He needs to find his king. And we need peace again in the Park.'

It was the rabbit who Rubic had met earlier.

'Perhaps I'd better introduce myself properly this time,' he said. 'I am Mitty of the Ancient order of the Warren. I have lived here all my life as did my forebears. We are descendants of the King's Warren. Our ancestors arrived with the Roman Legions. My kind have marched in many lands. We were there when the mountain buried the city. We were there when every town had a Roman garrison and a rabbit warren. We were there when the long straight roads were built.'

The rabbit paused, but only to take a breath.

Rubic was a polite fox, but knew he couldn't cope with a whole new tale of creature origins at this minute, and Mitty clearly hadn't finished, so he offered him what he knew of rabbits.

'And I've heard your kind helped raise the big stones,' he said.

'Well,' said Mitty. 'That is a nice story for the kits anyway. But where is the evidence, I ask? I could tell you ...'

But Rubic was still thinking about his Lady and his lost dream, rather than a lost king or rabbit ancestry. He interrupted.

'The deer,' he said, 'they are like the sheep on the Moor. They are farmed, not free.'

Mitty was distracted from history and replied.

'Of course they are. Few are free. We, the rabbits, we are free. You, the foxes, are free. The birds are free. That is obvious. What on earth have you been thinking?'

'It wasn't obvious to me,' said Rubic. 'I thought they were free creatures, running wild.'

'Never mind that now. Can you really find this lost King?'

'I don't know. But like I said I can try. And I can ask questions. You going to help?'

'If a fox and a rabbit can make a friendship, I am sure we can sort out the problems of the whole universe,' said Mitty.

'That Stella, that hind, she is so beautiful,' said Rubic.

'Well,' said the rabbit. 'Of course I like them. They are grass-eaters like us. But you?'

'I can't eat grass,' said Rubic, 'but I can't kill creatures either. That's why I came back to the city. You don't have to kill to eat in the city. And she has such beautiful eyes.'

'You're a bit smitten, aren't you? It is your own kind you are supposed to fall for. You need a mate, you do.'

'Well, I've never found one yet. It's all too complicated and I'm not sure about cubs. How can you teach cubs when you don't know the answers yourself?'

'Hmm. Plenty do,' said the rabbit. 'Anyway, this dead king …?'

'Do you think the Frenchies know anything?' said Rubic. 'But I can't talk to them.'

'It's La Reine we need,' said Mitty. 'She knows things and she'll talk to us, not like that nasty little buck of hers who will never get over the fact the red deer are called stags and are bigger than him. Doesn't know the meaning of manners, that creature.'

'Can I understand her?' said Rubic. 'Their talk is so funny.'

'Don't worry. I'll be there and you'll soon get the hang of it.'

'If we talk to her, by the time I go back to meet the Mareschalle to hear his side, then we might have some ideas,' said Rubic.

'We're in business,' said Mitty. 'I was getting a bit bored with life here anyway.'

16.
The Quest

La Reine was, as the rabbit said, a good source of information and, being a little ashamed of her mate's behaviour, she was anxious to hand on all she knew.

With Mitty translating where required, the fox and the rabbit discovered that the original story was much as Rubic had learnt on the Moor. The red deer saw themselves as the guardians of the King's Grave, but the last cull had taken them by surprise. They hadn't expected their leader to be taken before the secret was handed on to the next generation.

'He was just too clever, that last Mareschalle. He taught the young ones to open the gates into the new tree plantations. The two-leggeds, they watched and then they came and took him and his son. Any of us could have told him that sort of cleverness would lead to trouble.'

In the course of the conversation La Reine did say two things that were new to Rubic. She said

'When the Park was whole, before they cut it in half …' She was also clear that what the red stags had known was a secret about the King's Grave, not the whereabouts of the actual grave itself.

'If there was a grave here, we'd all know. This place isn't that big. The place they call the King's Mound isn't a grave, it is just where they used to go to stand and look at the city and, it was said they could see the King's Grave from there.'

The doe who had been chatting cheerfully to them suddenly raised her head. 'It's himself,' she said. 'I'll have to go. I have to keep him calm. He is getting agitated too. We don't want any more trouble.' She slipped quietly into the copse.

'We are finding out stuff,' said Rubic. '"When the park was whole …" We know who to ask about that. Let's go to the Wyche Tree and find Ned.'

Mitty had missed out on the meeting with the parakeet so he had to be filled in. 'Newcomers!' he said with a sniff.

'Everyone is a newcomer sometime,' said Rubic. 'I have learnt that. Come on. You coming?'

Back at the Wyche Tree, the two creatures looked around for the parakeet. It wasn't long before he appeared. He perched high up on the strange white dead thing that had become a shrine for so many different species.

'Thought you'd be back,' he said to Rubic. 'Brought a friend?'

'This is Mitty,' said Rubic. 'Things aren't right here.'

'You mean that big stupid beast charging around and upsetting everyone?' said the parakeet.

'Yes. Him. He says he has lost his secret. I've told his hind we'll find it.'

'I don't know anything about all that. My kind haven't been here long enough to know all the history.'

'We've found out some things,' said Rubic. 'The Frenchie doe, La Reine, she has told us. She said "When the Park was whole, they could see the King's Grave from the King's Mound."'

'You understood her?' said the bird. 'I surely can't.'

'It's only practice really,' said Mitty, 'but us rabbits are known to be the best linguists in the creature world.'

'Like I said before,' interrupted Rubic hastily, before Mitty could start on another of his tribal stories, 'it was your cousin Jendrix who found the way for us to the iron road. I sort of wondered if you could find the way for us here. You have wings. You could go look.' Rubic paused.

Ned the parakeet put his head on one side, scratched it with a claw and eyed the rabbit.

'One must be useful, I suppose,' he said. 'Then you all will be glad to have us newcomers.'

Mitty looked at Rubic.

'Everyone has to be a newcomer sometime,' said the rabbit.

Rubic was amazed. It was nice to be listened to occasionally.

'Alright I'll do the aerial survey for you. See you back here at dusk,' said Ned and flew off before Rubic could say any more.

'Now we have to be in two places at once said the fox. How can we meet the Mareschalle and see that parrot?'

'Don't panic,' said the rabbit. 'I can go find that stag and his missus and tell them you are coming. They won't eat me. Us grass-eaters can communicate. Meantime, let's go and look at this "King's Mound", see what is to be seen.'

The fox and the rabbit lolloped across the park and through the deer-proof fence. They left the wildish Moor and immediately were in cultivated gardens. Here there were well-behaved flowers, restrained and blooming in proper beds and lawns and little decorative brick walls. Following a brick path upwards, Mitty in the lead, the two creatures found themselves on a little hill of tarmac. Spread out below them was the landscape of southern England.

'Well, I suppose that stag could see lots from here, more than us, but he couldn't get up here, could he?' said Rubic. 'There's the fence.'

'It does look green down there and easy to explore,' replied the rabbit. 'But how on earth do we know where to go? I can smell the big water there, but we can't even see it from here.'

'What are we going to do?'

'You know,' said Mitty. 'We eat. We sleep. We wait till evening and see what that bird has found out. It was you who told me that we all need each other to get anything done.'

It seemed a good thought.

The beginnings of the cool of the evening found Rubic back at the Wyche Tree, waiting for Ned the parakeet. Mitty had gone to find the red deer stag and Stella his hind. Meanwhile things had been happening to Ned the parakeet.

17. Parakeets and Hawks

Ned's Adventure

'It'll be easy,' thought the parakeet. 'All I'll have to do is fly due west to the river and then follow it north. I'll soon see the other half of the Park.'

That is what the green bird did. In a few minutes he found himself flying north along the southern bank of the river Thames. He passed Glover's Island, following the river as it curved around. He watched briefly the busyness on Richmond Bridge. Beyond was another island and then the railway bridge over which Rubic and Charlie had travelled on their journey to the big city not so long ago. Beyond the railway bridge, almost immediately, Ned could see a second road bridge. Beyond that, at last, the green grass started.

Ahead of him was Richmond Lock, which is an

elaborate Victorian construction, recently updated to regulate London's river in digital times. There is only a footpath over the river but it is a very grand one. The bridge still has its fanciful towers and minarets and it was to the top of one of these Ned made his way.

'I'll be able to see everything from here,' he thought.

It was true. Perched on the top of one of the turrets, he could see for miles. More importantly for his mission, he could see a large undulating well-groomed patch of grass, slightly north and to the right of his perch.

Noise attracted his attention. He watched as a line of two-leggeds, in procession, marched their way across this grass towards the river. Some of them were making a weird sort of music he'd never heard before and all were wearing skirts.

As the parakeet watched, the leader, who was tossing a great stick into the air and catching it, shouted and the band of the Scots Guards (for that is who these two-leggeds were) halted in a semicircle around something that the bird couldn't see.

Behind the band came several small four-wheeled carts cruising over the grass. They drove to the inner part of the semicircle and their passengers got out.

Ned knew he had to get closer to see what was going on. He was drawn to this strange music. He took to his wings, flew towards the gathering and settled in a treetop from where he had a good view of what was going on below him.

There was some sort of ceremony. The parakeet was fascinated. The strange music continued. It crept into his head and he began to wonder if he could imitate it. As he listened, charmed and mesmerised, he saw various people lay things around a small white stone on the ground. The band stopped playing. Several two-leggeds made speeches.

After some time, everything seemed to be finished. A lone guardsman started once more to play the pipes. The parakeet listened. He was mesmerised by these single melancholy notes. He put his head back and concentrated all his brain on trying to reproduce the same sound.

Below him, the golf buggies containing the bigwigs turned themselves around and headed back the way they had come. The whole band followed. The last soldier was the lone piper still playing his pipes. Though Ned didn't know this, the tune was 'The Flowers of the Forest'.

The parakeet in the tree perched awhile, still captivated even as the bagpipe music faded. Finally there was silence. As soon as the marchers were far enough away he flew down to where this two-legged who had made these strange wonderful sounds had stood.

Ned understood something of what he had witnessed. That spot was obviously an important place. Still trying hard to make the strange sound, he flew over to the stone and started poking around the offerings laid there by the two-leggeds.

There was a circle of green leaves, a small golden crown, a sword and a belt with circular roundels on it. These attracted Ned and he pulled at them with his claws. It wasn't long before he had worked one loose. He held it in his claw. He strutted up and down in front of the memorial examining his stolen treasure and he continued to try to make the strange noises he had heard the piper make.

He completely forgot he was in strange territory and should have been watching out for himself. What he didn't know was that he had been observed. In the city and the airport it is now common to employ people with hawks to keep roofs and flight paths free of pigeons, gulls and any other birds seen as vermin. In London Town it is a business and livings are made at it.

Hawkers and their birds have to practice somewhere and today one such hawker was practicing on this golf-course. Ring-necked parakeets are not protected and those who believe in the importance of indigenous species rather than diversity applaud their culling.

The hawker saw the parakeet strutting around the memorial stone to James IV, the last king of Scotland, killed in battle on English soil. She saw the bird had taken something glittering from the ceremonial offerings.

She launched her own bird which was a Harris hawk. It flew up, circled and saw Ned the parakeet, his intended prey.

Ned remained unaware of the danger. He was struggling with how best to carry the brass roundel he had stolen from the ceremonial belt on the king's supposed grave.

He heard a sound and looked up. High above he could see the huge silhouette in the sky that would terrify any small bird anywhere on the planet. He could see broad wings and a broad tail and a head that he knew carried a cruel sharp beak, intended by nature for the ripping of flesh.

The hawk was overhead. Ned knew he was the target. He knew he'd better retreat, fast. He tried to fly up into a nearby tree, but his claw still compulsively gripped the brass roundel and so he was off balance.

Ned watched the hawk focus on him and begin its descent. The parakeet was paralysed with fear. He watched and couldn't move. It was the end for him, he knew that.

Then he heard, from above and behind him, a raucous hubbub. It was the sound of a flock of birds. It was the caws of corvids and the shrieks of parakeets, with each and every bird being as loud as it could. As Ned watched, the flock swept towards the hawk and surrounded it.

The hawk was flummoxed and harassed. This

didn't happen to him. He was a proper hunting hawk. He had targets and he achieved them and then deposited them at his handler's feet.

From below, Ned watched in amazement. The smaller birds continued to mob the hawk. They dived and circled and circled and dived. They completely prevented the raptor even seeing Ned the parakeet, his official target.

Below too, the handler watched in horror. This bird, her new hawk, was young and still learning. He couldn't possibly handle this sort of agro, she thought. He'd be put off hunting for ever. The handler put her whistle to her mouth and blew. She had to recall her bird now, immediately. It would never be able to work again if she didn't.

The bemused and confused hawk heard the call and flew upwards, over the trees and down with relief to the gloved arm the girl was holding out to him. She rewarded him with a small piece of meat from her bag as quickly as she could and made all the praising reassuring noises she could manage. The Harris hawk was glad to be safely home.

As she watched, the hawker saw the flock of birds dissipate. The jackdaws flew off towards the trees, but the parakeets, perhaps fifteen of them swooped down towards the ground all shrieking.

Ned saw them coming. He heard them shrieking as they swooped down. 'Cobber, cobber, cobber, maaaate,' they were calling.

He realised he'd been rescued by own kind. They surrounded him.

'Cmon, gotta move. Let's go.'

With the other green birds around him, now part of a flock, Ned rose with them. They all flew away together.

Rubic, waiting at the Wyche tree for the return of Ned, heard a fluttering and some squarking. He looked up. Not one but about twenty green parakeets were descending on the dead tree. They settled and perched and chittered to each other, while Rubic just looked on, astonished. Set against the grey dead branches they made a very beautiful picture.

'I've only ever seen one of you before,' he said.

A single bird emerged from the flock. It was Ned. He flew down to the ground, still with the round golden circle in his claw.

'Narrow escape,' he said.

With much interruption from the other parakeets, all of whom had something to say, the story was told.

'So,' said Rubic,' There is a sort of grave up there, to a king. And that sort of music, you say, comes from the North. And the two-leggeds were honouring him. And you've brought a relic. I wonder if that is enough?'

Rubic looked up at the flock of parakeets.

'Mitty, our rabbit colleague has gone to tell the Mareschalle and Stella we are coming,' he said.

'Let's go and take this story to them and see if that brings peace to the Park.'

Rubic looked at Ned the parakeet who was still clutching the heavy round boss in his claw.

'Want a ride?' he said. 'That looks awkward.'

The parakeets remained in the tree watching as one of their number rode on the back of a pale red fox as he walked the path towards the park. They realised it was a new sight. Maybe it meant new things.

Rubic's emotions, though he didn't know it, were those of a medieval troubadour. He loved his Lady Stella with the courtly passion of a medieval knight. As he trotted along he thought of her deep brown soft eyes. He would serve her. He so wanted to make her happy.

Ned however was simply amused.

'A funny old world,' he thought. He had watched two-leggeds riding four-legged horses in the park and here was he, a two-legged bird, travelling along on the back of a four-legged fox.

They had gone some considerable way into the park before the two found the Mareschalle and his herd. The big red stag was looking agitated and stamping his feet and shaking his great antlers about. He wasn't calm and relaxed. He looked extremely wound up.

'The gamekeeper had better not see him if he goes on like that,' said Ned. 'He looks as if he could attack anything. He looks really dangerous.'

'You mean?' said Rubic.

'Yes,' said Ned. They'll cull him. Can't have the public scared, you know.'

Stella was there. She was nuzzling the neck of her mate, but he wasn't responding. He tossed his head and pushed her aside and galloped down to the water's edge. He threw back his head and roared.

'Oh really,' said Ned. 'How stupid can you get?'

'Thank goodness you've come.'

Mitty the rabbit jumped out to greet them.

'We've got to do something pretty quickly. They won't let him carry on like that you know.'

'We can see that,' said Ned. 'What do you suggest?'

'Did you find anything?' asked the rabbit.

'Course I did. We're the Detectors, we are,' said Ned.

This was news to Rubic, but he rather liked the word. However, all three creatures were far more concerned with the emergency they could see happening in front of them.

'Mitty, you go and tell Stella we have news and we need to meet with her mate. Tell her it has to be in the trees, so we aren't so obvious. We are going over there. He needs to be got out of sight, quickly.'

Rubic gestured towards a copse that was dense enough to conceal them all. He and Ned set off for the wood. They found an open glade in the middle of the trees and settled themselves on the edge of the clearing. Ned deposited the brass circle with its Celtic symbol at Rubic's feet and flew up into a tree.

Before long there was a trampling and cracking of twigs and the Mareschalle entered the clearing. Close behind him was Stella, urging him on. Mitty brought up the rear. Rubic stood facing the clearly agitated Stag. He could see the whites of the creature's eyes as he tossed his head.

'Can we all sit?' he said. 'We have a story to tell you.'

There was a murmuring from Stella and finally the giant beast settled himself down. There was a sigh of relief from the other creatures present. Rubic began the conversation.

'We have found the burial place of your King,' he said.

'It is secret. I am the Guardian. You can't have,' said the Stag and then shaking his head, 'but I've lost it.'

He tossed his great antlers and moved to stand up. Stella leant out and nibbled his neck. Rubic went on quickly.

'I'm telling you,' he said 'We,' he paused and remembered the parakeet's word. 'We are Detectors. It is our job. We have found the grave for you.'

Ned let out a squawk and the stag looked up and saw him.

'Yes,' said Rubic. 'You couldn't guard it yourself. That is the secret you weren't told. It is in the other half of the park. Many years ago, the land was divided. My associate ...'

At this point Ned stalked up and down his branch,

bobbing his green head to the stag and Stella.

'My associate,' went on Rubic, 'will tell you his story.'

Ned flew down to the grass floor of the clearing and with the assistance of Mitty, who told of La Reine's contribution to the tale and also with an occasional bark of input from Rubic, told what he had seen.

'So you see,' said Rubic, 'the King isn't lost anymore. The two-leggeds have found him and made a proper memorial for him. That means your task is ended.'

The stag sat there and thought about this. Stella, his hind, turned her eyes to Rubic. She bowed her head to him and lowered her long dark eyelashes. Rubic felt his heart turn over as he looked at yet another 'Lady of his Dreams'.

Ned took up the tale again.

'We have brought you something from the grave. You can keep it here on this side of the park and tell your sons and they can tell their sons how the red deer kept the faith and guarded the King from the North until the two-leggeds found him again.'

Rubic, concentrating once more on the mission, lifted the round golden circle, carried it across the clearing and laid it in front of the seated stag. The stag bent his head and licked the yellow metal. He was silent, but as the other creatures watched, he grew calmer. Stella licked his neck again. The parakeet chittered quietly in Rubic's ear.

'See, see, he doesn't look mad any more.'

Rubic said nothing. He didn't need to.

The stag looked at Mitty. He seemed majestic once more. He spoke to the rabbit.

'You are a grass-eater, so one of us. Will you help? We need to bury this treasure, this relic somewhere safe, somewhere the follow-ons can visit and hear the story of their heritage.'

Stella, his mate, looked into his face. If deer could smile she did. She bowed her head to him. He stood up. She did too. She first licked his neck and then the yellow circle he held in his mouth, but this time it wasn't the nibbling lick of an anxious nurse, but the appreciation of a beloved spouse.

Rubic watched the stag and Stella walk away followed by Mitty the rabbit. He knew, really, he was a fox, but he had loved Stella, the red deer hind in some complicated way and now he could see she only had eyes for her stag. He didn't follow the deer. He just lay on the grass and thought.

'What about that other dream, to run with deer in freedom?' The fox bent his head as he considered. 'These deer aren't free to run, like those on the Moor. They really are farmed, even if it isn't polite to say so. Has this journey all been for nothing?

'And yet,' he said to himself, 'I have seen things and done things and know more things than I did when I left the Moor. Is that good? Or am I just a sadder fox?'

He wasn't even sure if the way the deer lived was bad, or whether it was just another way of being. None of this was easy. The one thing he did know was that this place wasn't for him. If they culled deer they probably culled foxes too. That was why he hadn't seen any of his own kind. It had been a dream, but not a dream that could become reality. He had not found his place. He had to move on.

To this day, when visiting Richmond Park, if you see the red deer congregating together in a particular place, they well may be paying their respects to the brass roundel that Mitty and his relations buried so carefully for them in the deepest of rabbit burrows. They might be making sure the next generation know the story of how the red deer completed their mission to guard the grave of the Scottish King until he was rediscovered by the two-leggeds.

18.
New Friends Make New Plans

Rubic and Mitty and Ned met again later that evening beside the Wyche Tree. Each had been off to find their own food, but now it seemed it was the time for talking.

The rabbit and the parakeet were deep in conversation when Rubic arrived. They looked at him.

'We are going into business,' said the rabbit.

'We are the Detectors,' said the parakeet.

They both looked at the fox.

'And you're not going to join us, are you?' said Mitty.

'No,' said Rubic. 'I have to go home.'

'But the Running? That was the point, I thought. You ran away from your home,' said Ned.

'Only for Blackberry. To save him. Don't you see? I have to go back – to tell the story to my tribe.'

'They'll know by now anyway. The green birds ...' said Mitty.

'But not from me. Not from me.'

There was a pause. Silence. Rubic looked at these, the newest friends of the many he'd made on his journey.

'Tell me about your Plan,' he said.

'Well,' replied Ned the parakeet. 'We've been talking. There are always problems here in the Park. As we know big things get lost, but little things also. In spring cubs and kits go wandering and they have to be found. And someone must keep an eye on the two-legged bosses all the time. We need to know what they are up to.'

'And the visitor two-leggeds,' added Mitty. 'Some stuff they leave is great to eat, but some like those plastic bags do the calves and fawns no good at all. There needs to be watching, detecting and finding if required. Creatures are needed to do it. And they are going to be us.'

'But the others,' said Rubic. 'What do they say?'

'After what you made happen, sorting the Mareschalle out like that, so they didn't take him away. Finding out the story. Everyone, even the Frenchies understand we must have ways of sorting things out.'

'Ways?' said Rubic.

'Ways of talking and deciding and creatures who will do things. Detectors.'

'And we are the first in the Park,' said Mitty.

Rubic was startled. This reminded him of what happened at Stonehenge. When Buckfast the rabbit suddenly became a leader and called the first Rabbitting. Everyone seemed to think that he, Rubic, had had a hand in all that, and now, again, they seemed to think he'd done something important.'

'It wasn't me. I just came,' said Rubic. 'I was looking for the free deer.'

'Yes,' said Ned, 'But without you it wouldn't have happened at all.'

'You changed things, us,' said Mitty. 'If you are going to leave us, we must help. What can we do?'

'You need a Plan too,' said Ned.

'Well,' said Rubic. 'There is something you could do for me. I've been thinking too.

Just over the road, outside the Park there is a feline. He lives in a place called a church. It is near the iron road. I need one of you to go and talk to him. His name is Charlie and he does know the words. I met his mother.'

'What shall we say?'

'Just tell him the story and say I need to catch a train back to the Place of the Dead, another one, like the one here, but where my tribe live. He is very young still but, hopefully he has learnt enough by now to arrange it.'

'And if he hasn't?'

'Well, I had another thought. There is one other who

knows where I came from. He is one of your kind, Ned. You said you'd heard of him. Jendrix, he was called.'

Ned looked a little uncomfortable.

'Yes I've heard of him, he said. But he is very important. Lives in Kew Gardens. He has certainly never heard of me. They say he was the first of our kind to go to the North up the Hill.'

'Of course he was! That was to see us,' said Rubic. 'He was the first green bird we'd ever seen up there. Listen, can you get a message to him?'

'I suppose I could, but will he listen?'

'Tell him that Rubic of the Running, brother of Butch the Navigator, needs his help. He will help, I am sure.'

Ned shifted from foot to foot, looking anxious.

'Listen,' said Rubic, 'we all make history, we just don't know we are doing it till afterwards. Jendrix came to us foxes because he got a message saying he should. He was just a young bird then and cocky with it. He and my brother Butch made maps in their heads and that's what made the longest Running ever happen. Now maybe he is famous, but he is just another green bird really.'

Ned still looked dubious. Rubic had another thought.

'And I bet he could give you some advice about being a Detector,' he said. 'He had burglars as helpers.'

Ned looked curious.

'Squirrels. They are good with their paws. There are lots of them here. Maybe you could sign them up.'

Mitty butted in.

'Useless lot. Not a single brain between them all. They just leap and chatter all day.'

'And steal our eggs,' added Ned.

'Until someone tells them new things, new ways,' said Rubic. 'Hearing new things is what I've done. It has made me ...' he paused, 'bigger.'

'Hmm,' said the parakeet, 'Bigger, says who? Just look at you! One ear missing and half-starved. Not a pretty picture.'

Rubic was cross.

'Well bigger in the head then. I know things now. I've seen things.'

'He is right, you know,' said Mitty. 'We need ideas. Before he came, I was getting fed up. Now we have found something to do to make our place better. Us rabbits ...' he began.

With one accord, both Rubic and Ned barked and quarked. They knew they had to stop Mitty before he got started!

The rabbit did stop. He sat back on his hind legs and started grooming his ears with his paws.

'Alright, he squeaked. 'I know I go on a bit, but it can be useful. You know it can. In the end I am listened to. I had to go on and on to get the Mareschalle to listen.'

The three creatures remained quiet for a while in the twilight, enjoying the bond between them. Eventually Ned spoke first.

'Alright, tomorrow at first light I will go to Kew gardens and enquire for Jendrix and give him the message. And this time I shall watch carefully for those hawks.'

'And I,' said Mitty, 'I will go and see if I can find this Charlie. At least I know how to do it without crossing that Road.'

Rubic realised all of a sudden that both his friends were prepared to put themselves at risk for him. A little ashamed he barked his goodnight to them, put his paws over his nose and fell asleep.

The following morning both the creature friends set out on their respective missions. Mitty's turned out to be the easiest. His secret way over the road was in fact under it. A drain led him beneath the traffic directly to the church yard. From the shrubbery within the fence, he watched for a while the antics of a rather stringy, long-haired and obviously young tabby feline.

Thinking he was unseen, Charlie was chasing flies. He leapt up into the air, fell back down, rolled around on the grass and even chased his own tail. He was in fact behaving like the kitten he had so recently been.

Mitty, from the safety of the bushes, squeaked the word.

'Pax, Pax,' he called.

Charlie stopped dead in mid-cavort. He landed on all fours, stood still and listened.

Mitty repeated himself.

'Pax, Pax.'

'Fainites, fainites,' came the reply. Mitty, not ever having spoken to a cat before, because they were never allowed into the Park, could just about understand what was said. He came out from under the bush.

'I bring a message, he said. From a friend of yours, a fox called Rubic,' he said.

Charlie, being a country cat by birth understood the rabbit talk.

'Is he well? Did he find his heart's desire? Is he free?'

'None of those, really,' replied Mitty. 'But can we find somewhere a bit less open?'

'Oh sorry, said the cat. 'I still forget the two-leggeds wouldn't get it. Me talking to you, I mean. Follow.'

They settled down in a quiet corner out of sight of all.

Mitty told his story, with, for him, a minimum of side trips and tales of rabbit heroes of the past. Charlie being young and well brought up and less experienced in the ways of the world, listened with patience. In consequence he learnt more than he expected.

Mitty too, having no experience of cats was charmed by this young, rather nervous feline, who was so anxious to please. Eventually, having told each other many stories, they got down to the matter in hand.

'Can you help our Rubic get on the iron road back to his birthplace in the North of the city?' asked Mitty.

'Look,' said Charlie,' I'm pretty new at all this. I haven't had to arrange transport or anything yet. My boss comes by every week or two to check on me and anything complicated he deals with.

I could do it, get him on a train, if someone told me which one, but I don't know the ways and the tracks and the timetables. I haven't had time to learn.'

'Well that's a start,' said Mitty. 'We've got someone else looking into the routes. Someone is contacting the Big Cat.'

Charlie was a little shocked.

'You're talking of Skimble Twelve of Paddington?' he said. 'The Feline Senior.'

'Er, yes,' said Mitty, amused by Charlie's reverence.

'You mean I might get a message from him? He might actually be told of me?' asked Charlie.

'Very likely, I'd say,' said Mitty.

Charlie was silent for a bit.

'I hope my mother gets to hear,' he said.

'What I think will happen,' went on the rabbit, 'is that a green bird will come with a message. Then you will know what to do.'

'A message from Him,' said Charlie wonderingly.

Mitty hadn't the patience for this mystical reverence. If anything he was a republican rabbit and didn't approve of royalty.

'Listen,' he said. I must get back before the world wakes up. Be alert. You'll hear. And Cheers.'

Before Charlie could respond properly to the formal farewell, Mitty had hopped off into the trees, back to his drain pipe, under the road and back into the Park.

19. Ned Meets His Hero

Meanwhile Ned too was off to get help. Kew Gardens, or as they are more properly known 'The Royal Botanical Gardens, Kew', aren't far from Richmond Park. Both are tucked within a bend of the River Thames on the western side of London. Kew Gardens was in fact just north of the golf course where Ned had found the grave of the lost king and had his encounter with the hawk. This time, however, he flew in that direction with great caution and kept all his wits about him.

The boundary between the golf course and Kew Gardens was obvious. Bare green grass and hummocks suddenly became copses of interesting trees. There were flowerbeds and a lake and an extraordinary curved glass house that glittered in the sun as Ned approached it.

He was wondering how to find his relatives, but he needn't have done so. There was a quark from a nearby tree.

'It's the bird who loves the bagpipes!'

'Got yourself some specs?'

'Seen any good hawks lately?'

'Hey, you old enough to be out on your own?'

It isn't considered necessary to use the Words within your own species so Ned landed on a branch of the tree from which all the comments were coming.

'Oy,' he replied, 'I know, I know, but I was working, not just sitting in a tree, like you lot, shouting rude remarks at passers by.'

There was more rather rude conversation between the birds, which it isn't necessary to relate here. With their own kind, parakeets do not pull their punches. To a bystander their conversation sounds like simple abuse.

Eventually, all having exhausted their repertoire of taunts and teases, conversation moved on to the matter in hand.

'I've come with a message for Jendrix from an old friend of his,' said Ned. 'How do I find him?'

'Ah, Jendrix, Jendrix,' chattered the parakeets. There was a little more respect in their reply to their visitor. 'He'll be in the Spa at this time of day.'

'The Spa?' queried Ned.

Various parakeet voices replied.

'Well, he is quite an old bird now and it helps the arthritis.'

'He can get in when the gardeners go in, and has

an hour's therapy,'

'He leaves before they shut the ventilators.'

'Has to be careful though.'

'We keep watch for him.'

'He is the Jendrix after all.'

Ned had no idea what these birds were talking about and said so.

'We'll show you, come on.'

A flock of green parakeets rose from the tree and Ned was one of them. They flew towards the giant glass house that Ned had seen on his way in. The birds settled on the roof ridge and one of their number paced along to meet another bird coming towards him. The nearest bird to Ned leant over and gently pecked his neck.

'See,' she said, 'look, down, underneath.'

Ned did as he was bidden.

Beneath him inside the great glass house he could see lots of lush greenery of a kind he'd never seen growing in the Park.

'See him?' said his guide.

Ned couldn't.

'Look again, there, on that palm tree.'

Ned looked and finally saw.

What he saw was a rather large green parakeet with a beautifully developed black face mask and neck ring.

The bird was flapping each wing in turn. As Ned watched, the bird walked out along a branch of the palm, stretching and bending each claw and twisting his neck as far as it would go.

'What's he doing? Is that Jendrix?' asked Ned. 'And why is he in there?'

The bird that had walked along the ridge had now returned and overheard the remark.

'His Tai Chi. You'll see,' she said. 'Follow me.'

The bird led Ned down the side of the roof of the glass house. There was a small pane of glass tilted at an angle.

'Through there,' said his guide. 'And it's hot in there. He is expecting you.'

Ned hadn't realised what he was in for. He climbed through the ventilator and was hit by a wave of heat such as he'd never experienced before. It took his breath away. He faltered in his attempt to scramble down the iron trellis work of the greenhouse to the palm tree where Jendrix was exercising.

'Hold up, hold up,' he heard.

A moment later he was on another palm frond nodding his head to a green parakeet that was at least twice his size.

'Yeah, bit of a surprise at first isn't it? I'm told this is what it is like in our original birth land. Very good for my wing joints, this heat.'

Ned hadn't yet spoken. Jendrix went on.

'So you're the Bagpipe Bird, hmmm?'

'My name is Ned, sir,'

'Well, I think you'll find you've a new moniker

now,' said Jendrix.

'Ned I've always been sir, and Ned I'll stay.'

'You can try,' said Jendrix. 'Anyway, glad you came. I have heard the stories of course, but I'd like to hear your version. How is that fox? I didn't expect to see him again.'

'Couldn't say he was happy, sir.'

'We don't "sir" – we are birds,' said Jendrix.

'Sorry, It's just ...'

'Rubic. He isn't the one I thought I'd see again. Maybe the foreign one or the Navigator, but not that pale one.' Jendrix realised he was talking to himself. 'Anyway, tell me: what does he want to do next?'

'He says he needs to go home, to take the stories back.'

'Yes, I can understand that.'

'But he doesn't know the right train to take.'

'Ah the Big Cat. We need his help.'

'I've heard of him. There is a young tabby cat, Charlie, who calls him Skimble Twelve.'

'Indeed, indeed. Yes, that is his name, but to most of us he is the Big Cat. He knows it all.'

Jendrix continued to stretch each wing in turn, flexing and twisting his neck as he did so. Ned watched in amazement, then remembering what had been said:

'All?' he asked.

'He is the master of the Permanent Way. He knows track and train, times and traffic. All there is to know about the iron road, the freedom road, he knows it.

'I think getting a fox from Richmond to Highgate will be a very small task for him.'

'It will?'

'Oh yes. It really isn't far you know, even for a four-legged. The big Cat, he sends things hundreds of miles and gets things back too. They say he gets sent Cornish pilchards from the south and a Haggis at New Year. He had contacts everywhere. We'll need to send a message. Not good for us parakeets to be seen in the city centre. Don't want to advertise.

I'll send a pigeon. That's what always used to be done. Trouble is it is becoming dangerous for them too. The two-leggeds seem to have decided they are a bad thing.'

'Pigeons?' said the smaller parakeet incredulously.

'They are supposed to make the two-leggeds sick. It is a new thing. They are so fickle those two-leggeds. It'll be us next, you'll see. Low profile essential.'

The reader, if a Londoner, might wonder how on earth a parakeet could adopt a low profile given their visibility and the noise they make.

'Anyway that's a problem for another time. Today a single pigeon can still walk along the platform at Paddington without causing a fuss.'

'So, Mr Jendrix, what do I tell Charlie and them back in the Park?'

'I said, didn't I? Just Jendrix. We don't do titles. And I think we'd better move out of here. My time is up. Listen, they are closing the ventilators, follow me.'

Very swiftly, the bigger bird flew up to the glass roof, walked along an iron strut to an open glass pane. He slipped through, out into the open air. Ned followed him as quickly as he could, but again faltered when, as he came through the glass pane, the cold outside air hit him.

'How do you manage?' he gasped.

'It's very good for you. Good for the lungs,' said the big bird as he perched on the ridge of the great glass house, flapping and spreading his green wings so that both the blue and yellow feathers of his plumage could be seen.

Ned rapidly adapted once more to the outside air, but remained unconvinced as to the benefits of Spa indulgence.

'As I was saying,' went on Jendrix, 'You go back. Tell that tabby feline Charlie to watch for a messenger. A creature will need to visit him every day from the Park to check.'

'So he'll be getting a message from the Big Cat?'

'Of course. How else do you think ...?'

'He will be pleased. My rabbit friend says he wants his mother to know. We think he is a bit lonely in the city.'

'Hmm, I'll pass that on too. Felines can easily send a message down the line. We must all look after each other.'

Ned returned to the Park, to the Wyche Tree without incident. He perched on its top branch and waited. Before long both Rubic and Mitty appeared and he told his tale.

'You mean I have to go under that road every day to see that cat?' said Mitty.

'Actually, I don't see why I shouldn't go sometimes,' said Ned. 'We know he knows the words and I'm a bit more careful now.'

Rubic listened quietly. He was leaving again. These, his newest friends seemed very keen to organise his departure. Perhaps they would be glad to see him go? Then he remembered that it was he who wanted to leave and was rejecting their world. He looked at Mitty and Ned.

'I'm sorry,' he said.

'No,' said Mitty, who understood instantly. 'You are wrong. It is just that we can see you are sad. You have brought peace to this place and we want you to be happy and be peaceful too. So we want to do all we can to help you find your place to be.'

It was reassuring. Rubic recalled one of his grandmother's sayings: 'A rolling stone gathers no moss.' Was he that? A rolling stone. Just always moving on? He seemed to have gathered quite a lot of moss along the way if you considered all the new creatures he'd met and the scars he he'd got from the stoats and weasels.

He knew, though he hadn't finished his search or found his place, he had to move on. And the next place to go was his beginning place. He could tell his stories and perhaps understand what he had to do next.

20. Homeward Bound

There was a lot of aerial to-ing and fro-ing during the following week between Paddington Station and Richmond Park and Charlie the cat in the church grounds.

It transpired that the new overground trains were difficult for non-humans to get in and out of because the doors didn't always open automatically at every station. They also had seats down each side rather than arranged in pairs facing each other. This meant there were few areas for creatures to lurk unnoticed. In addition, the trains had no guard's van. Thus it was decided that Rubic should catch an old-fashioned London Underground tube train from Richmond Station, going on the District Line to Paddington. From there he could follow the route of the original Runners, back the way they came, up the canal, along the railway line, through the park and finally to his birthplace, Highgate Cemetery.

'We'll sort out a guide to go with him on the tube,' came the message. 'The fox must be at Richmond tube station before midnight to catch the last train east.'

Charlie was detailed to lead Rubic to the station. Late one dark night, as the last of the revellers were making their way home, the fox slipped out of Richmond Park. Mitty the rabbit went with him to the edge of the grass while Ned watched from the topmost branch of a nearby tree.

Their visitor was going. He'd altered their lives. He'd brought peace. He'd helped them forge a new alliance between the creatures of the Park that it was hoped would stand them in good stead in the future.

Rubic too had his thoughts. This had been another dream that hadn't worked out for him. He knew he had to go. He hadn't found his own place. He didn't say the formal goodbye words, to his new friends. He wasn't sure why he didn't. He just quietly left the Park the way he had come. He crossed the road and met Charlie in the church grounds. Charlie was looking nervous but rather pleased with himself and somehow more confident.

'I got a message from down the line from my mother,' he said. 'She was very pleased and is telling my story at the next Moonmeet.'

Rubic knew that Ned had mentioned this young cat Charlie to Jendrix and was delighted that inter-species creature communications had worked so well. Charlie continued to talk.

'What we've got to do is this. We follow these rails into the station. A creature there will meet us and take you to the small red trains whose doors always open. He will go with you to the big station where the Senior Feline, Skimble Twelve, lives. I have been told that there is no need for you to go too far into the station. The little red trains stop near the canal. Once you find the canal bank, they say you know the way.'

'What creature will be at the station?' asked Rubic.

'I don't know,' said Charlie. 'We just have to keep our eyes open. But he is an experienced traveller on the tube, I'm told.'

It wasn't difficult to trek through the allotments back to the railway line where Charlie and Rubic had originally arrived in the city. As they trotted along, Rubic asked a question.

'Why can't I just jump a train from here?' asked Rubic. 'Why do we have to go into the station? Surely there are two-leggeds there?'

'Different line, I'm told. We go in and then you get on another kind of train that comes out on another set of tracks and will take you to Paddington Station and the canal path which they say you should know from before.'

The station was lit. They could see the platform edge. They crept up the slope where it met the track and onto the platform itself.

The only creatures visible were a pair of pigeons billing and cooing to each other. Charlie eyed them predatorily, then remembered he was on a mission. The birds saw the fox and the cat and stopped cooing at each other. What the new arrivals heard was a loud cheep. It was clearly interpretable as 'Pax'.

'Fainites,' Rubic replied, somewhat startled to hear the word from a pigeon. 'You the guide?' he asked incredulously.

If creatures understood accents, they would have realised that the pigeons were born within the sound of Bow Bells. They were cockney birds.

'Oy mate and why not?' said the cock.

'Been in this city longer than your lot,' said the hen bird, 'and two-leggeds don't notice us, unlike those flashy avians you've been mixing with lately.'

Rubic remembered his manners.

'So sorry,' he said. 'I've been away. Don't see many of your kind on the Moor. Of course you are the bird of the city. Your kind can go anywhere.'

Both birds cooed their acknowledgement of his apology. The hen bird looked at the cock.

'Off now. Work to do. See y' later.' She spread her wings and disappeared into the dark sky.

'No one ever chases us pigeons when they think we are courting,' said the cock bird. 'Just acting up. She's my sister, Hat. I'm Sid. Now, we gotta get right down the platform to the end.

'Cat you'd better disappear. Y'job's done. Us'ld be noticed. You are s'posed to chase me!'

Charlie didn't want to quit this new adventure, but could see the point. He turned to Rubic.

'Good to meet you, sir. Will you tell my story to any of my kind you meet?'

Rubic had developed an affection for this young creature trying so hard to make his way in the world without friends and family nearby.

'Of course I will. Where I am going we have Sister Cat, who saved my brother Blackberry when he was a cub. She shall hear of you. Now it's the time. Cheers mate.'

Charlie paused, thought and then remembered his line.

'A safe run and good speed,' he said. Then he faded, almost invisibly, off into the darkness.

'He is still very young,' remarked Rubic to the pigeon.

'Crew, crew,' said Sid the pigeon. 'Nah cats. Claws! C'mon. Keep low, and to the side.'

The bird stalked up the edge of the platform towards the concourse. It was almost empty at 11.30 at night. Rubic, as he was told, followed him, slinking up the inner side of the station, against the wall.

The bird walked across the open concourse and set off down another platform to the end. Rubic had no choice but to follow. He crept along as unobtrusively as he could. Both creatures reached the end of the platform safely. The pigeon settled under a bench.

'Stay 'ere,' he cheeped. 'Won't be seen.'

Rubic looked around. He realised he wasn't far from the end of the very platform he had just climbed onto with Charlie.

'But why didn't we just walk across?'

'Leccy rails,' said the bird. 'Didn't know if you'd deal. Me, I just fly across.'

Rubic wasn't sure he understood this, but had learnt in his journeying that locals usually knew best.

'What now?'

'Wait. District line. First carriage. Doors open. In quick. Lie low. Between seats. Change at Earl's Court.'

This was all largely incomprehensible to Rubic. This bird was a complete contrast to Mitty. Whenever that rabbit had started speaking, the listener soon realised that he would have to interrupt to get a word in edgeways. A few more words from this bird, thought Rubic, would help.

'You coming too?' was all he asked.

'Course. Have to change. Pie eaters OK with us on the tube. We're just pigeons y'know.'

Something clicked in Rubic's head. He remembered the talk from when he was a cub. He remembered his cousin Pearl, from the east of the city, who, as was said then, 'had come shopping on the Northern Line,' but had ended up staying with the Highgate foxes. He remembered his own name.

'I'm Rubic,' he said.

'Yeah, they said. Won't croak to nosh. Y'e like a Ruby. Done a bunk. Couldn't live with the hayseeds.'

The fox suddenly understood his own language again. Home was home. He was a city fox, but mostly he was a Londoner.

There was the rumbling noise of an approaching train

'Cmon don't want to miss the Michael.'

Readers who are not Londoners might like a translation. It is as follows: 'They said you wouldn't kill other creatures to eat. You like a curry. You ran away because you didn't like the country folk.'

'Shopping on the northern line' is a phrase used by both human and vulpine young from East London referring to street robberies of their cousins in the richer northern parts of the city such as Hampstead and Highgate.

'The Michael' is rhyming cockney slang for train: Michael Caine = train.

The final carriage of the red train drew to a halt in front of them. The doors opened. Sid stalked showily across the platform, hopped up and in. He turned his head and cheeped. Rubic ran low and fast and followed him into the carriage.

'Down, 'tween th' seats,' said Sid. 'Empty. Fine.'

It was a few minutes before this, nearly the last train of the day, departed. The fox and pigeon were in what would now become the first carriage, as it headed east towards central London.

As they lay still they heard the driver walk up the platform, unlock his driver's compartment and get into the train. There was a noise as all the doors shut and then smoothly moved off.

This front carriage of the train was a long way down the platform, and few late night travellers could be bothered to walk that far, thus as Sid said, the two creatures had it to themselves.

The train travelled east, stopping at every station and for a while the two creatures remained undisturbed. At Hammersmith a man stumbled into their carriage. He was perhaps a little worse for wear.

'Had a few,' said Sid, 'Nah problem. Change soon.'

Rubic remained flat on the floor between the bench seats, not daring to raise his head.

'Don't panic,' said Sid. ''E won't believe it if he does spot you. Drink taken.'

The train moved off again, the doors opened and shut twice more.

'Next stop,' said the pigeon. 'Follow.'

Not entirely sure what to do, Rubic did as he was told.

At the next stop, as the doors opened, the pigeon stalked out. Rubic followed.

'Down 'ere,' said Sid.

Rubic found they were hiding under a broad

staircase. He didn't know it, but it led up to the concourse and the street.

'Wait. Need Circle Line.'

Another red train came in and left.

'What was wrong with that one?' asked Rubic.

'Not f'r us.'

'How can you tell?'

'Stay. Show you.'

The bird flew up and along the platform and settled on a gantry which ran across the station. Below him on a display board were a set of indicator arrows pointing at destination names. The arrow at the bottom of the board lit up as the bird landed. Rubic watched. Sid flew back to the fox.

'Next one. Us.'

'Did you do that? Make the light come on?'

'Nah, course not. Bottom signal is the one for the Big Cat's station. It's lit so next train's ours. Follow. Won't be so easy.'

It was only three stations to Paddington. During the journey, Sid explained to Rubic how he was going to get him over the last lap of this journey to the canal bank.

'Just one lot apples and pears. All kosher. Me, I fly, then perch. You run. I fly on. You follow. Got it? Pie eaters will watch me, not you.'

The strategy worked. All Rubic remembered afterwards was a series of tiled passages, then the huge open space of the station. He focussed his eyes firmly on the bird as it flew and perched and flew and perched on each set of railings. Finally, there was a long straight run with a left turn at the end of it. Rubic ran. As he turned left he smelt water and sure enough there in front of him was the darkness of the canal glistening as street lights were reflected off its surface.

Sid landed and perched on the wall outside the station.

'Phew,' he said. 'Wasn't sure we were going to pull that off. Had the flock ready for an emergency call out, but we managed!'

Rubic lay down on the canal bank and put his nose between his paws. He too was relieved to be out of the station.

'Y' know your way from here, they say. I'll be off. Gotta get back. Good speed.'

'Cheers mate,' said Rubic as the pigeon flew up over the station roof and disappeared.

The fox was about to turn left along the canal, the way he had come all those months ago when he heard a squeak.

'Nooo. Too much traffic. We go the other way.'

He paused and searched through his memory. There were so many creatures in it now, since his adventures began.

'Greetings Hamlin,' he said. 'Pax.'

'Fainites, ' came the reply. 'Didn't think to see you again or, come to that, that you'd remember one rodent.'

'I do remember, and I do know the way from here,' said Rubic.

'Found a better,' said the brown rat. 'Other side. Easier at the junction. Don't want you ending up in Greenford.'

'I'm not my brother,' said Rubic, thinking of Butch. 'He was the curious one.'

'Yes, I remember him. Strange fox.' The rat paused a moment and looked hard at Rubic. 'You've been in the wars, you have. Not sure your own mother would know you now!'

Rubic had forgotten he might not be the same fox who had left the city, a foxling, all that time ago.

'I hope she does,' was all he said.

Hamlin the rat didn't reply. He was concentrating on getting this rather battered fox where he wanted him.

'Now, see that little bridge, just along there, to the left. We are going over that.

He suited his actions to his words.

'And now round these buildings and we'll be back on the canal bank.'

Rubic followed.

'I'll leave you here. It's easy now. You stay by the water. Not so many live in boats on this side. Go under the bridge, past the puppet theatre ...'

'Puppet theatre?' Rubic interrupted. 'What's that?'

'You know, where the two-leggeds tell their stories. Just like us creatures do. But they need these little wooden people to help them. Anyway, it will be closed for the night now, so it will be quiet. You just stay on that side, like I said, past the puppet theatre and then through the two-leggeds' flower garden until you come to the end. Your bit of waterway turns there. Follow it till you come to the Zoo.'

Hamlin suddenly looked bothered.

'You will be okay, won't you? I am sorry I really do have to go now. I am expected. Many of my kind have had to move because of the big new underground tunnel. I am part of the guiding committee. Resettling friends and relations isn't easy.'

'Ah,' said Rubic, 'a sort of Running? Like ours?'

'Well,' said the rat. 'There were only seven of you. There are thousands of us displaced by these new diggings.'

This gave Rubic a moments pause. So his kind weren't the only creatures forced by circumstances to move.

'Things change, the world changes,' said the rat. 'We just have to adapt. But I will say that seven foxes were easier to relocate than thousands of kin. Really must go now. You will be fine. Good speed and a safe haven.'

'Cheers,' said Rubic.

Hamlin disappeared through a fence. Rubic heard a small splash as the rat disappeared into the water and swam away.

21. The Last Lap

The fox was alone for the first time for a while. He followed Hamlin through the fence and was on the canal bank. It was easy to trot along the water's edge, even in the darkness. He'd had good instructions. He recognised the puppet theatre by the pennants outside it. They were drooping on this windless night. He could see where the people went up the steps and in to watch the show.

Beyond that there was grass and then the formal gardens with their gravel paths. The canal broadened out. Rubic could see an island. He recognised it as, where on his last visit the bird with the hooked beak had squawked directions. Just beyond the island he could see that there was a junction, one canal became two, but for Rubic there was no confusion. The rat had been clear. He was to follow the one on his side and he would reach the Zoo.

It wasn't really very far. Rubic had done it before. Past the big iron cage he went. He heard the strange sounds of the wild dog puppies and watched the parents herd their young under cover.

As he trotted on along the canal bank he felt the temperature drop. The grass became crunchy under his paws. He padded on a little further. Snow began to fall. It was just a few flakes at first, which swirled around and melted into the canal. Gradually the snowflakes got bigger and bigger and began to settle.

Rubic had become a thin fox. He hadn't eaten well for some time and he'd been ill. The icy wind went through his coat and he shivered. He had to lift his paws high to walk through the deepening snow. He left a trail of paw prints along the canal edge.

His main worry was whether he would know when to leave the canal and join the railway. The last time he had been here, his cousin Butch and his mother Rubia had scent-marked the route, but this time he would have to find his own way and this time he was doing it backwards. Last time there had been the fleecy greenery of summer. This time it was winter and he was cold and tired and everything looked different.

In the end, the problem solved itself. There was a thundering and a train bright with light went over the canal on a bridge just ahead of him. This was his bit of iron road, he knew it. He waited till the train had gone and climbed up the side of the canal bridge to the railway embankment. Ahead of him was the track. He knew he had to go north which was uphill if he was to find his way home to Highgate.

On he went, along the gravel by the side of the rails. There was less snow there. The tracks suddenly multiplied, but Rubic could see where to go. He watched for the city farm animals, but the shed doors were shut and all was quiet under the thickening blanket of snow.

The fox was confident he knew his way. The track he had to follow seemed, to his eyes to stand out from all the others around him. In the end, it is always easy to find your way home. Before too long he saw the place where he had to leave the rails and descend into the park where the two-legged played their games. The snow was even thicker on the lower ground.

As he plodded through it, his head became filled with more and more questions. Why was he here? What would his relations say? His mother Rubia. Had she ever got home after biting the two-legged at the station? And his father, what about him? And above all, what was he, Rubic supposed to be doing? Where was he supposed to be?

Rubic may have been confident of his route, but he wasn't strong. The thick snow was a problem for him. Small drifts began to build up. They would have been little trouble to normal-sized two-leggeds, but they hindered the progress of an underfed fox.

He struggled on, but by the time he reached the

bottom of the park where the road led uphill to his final destination, the snow was brushing his stomach. He knew that just at the top of this road were the railings that bordered the churchyard that was his birthplace. That was home. He stopped to rest.

He lay down. It wasn't a good idea to stop moving. He knew that, but it seemed too much trouble to move. He settled in the snow and shut his eyes.

'In a moment I'll move on,' he said to himself.

He heard a rustling nearby and then Rubic felt himself being shoved – that was the only word for it, shoved, by something much heavier than himself.

He opened one eye, lifted his head and then looked with both eyes. There was a big solid shape in the snow looking back at him.

'Uncle Cousin!' said Rubic.

'So you haven't forgotten us,' said the badger. 'Now move, young one, move. I will go in front and you will follow. It will be easier.'

For good measure he gave Rubic another hefty shove in the hind quarters.

'Got it? Now move.'

The fox really had no choice with the snout of a large badger pushing at his rump. He got up onto his four legs. The badger turned and set off up the snow-covered pavement. As he went, his broad body cleared the snow and left a path which it was easy for Rubic to follow.

It was only a matter of minutes before the black

iron railings of the cemetery came in sight.

'Through with you,' said the badger. 'They're waiting.'

Rubic slipped through. Before he had walked even five paces there was a yelping.

'It's him, it's him,' Rubic could hear. A shape appeared in front of him and he heard more words. 'Pax, brother.'

Rubic just managed to give his reply, 'Fainites', before he collapsed.

The next thing he remembered was being warm and out of the snow. He could hear foxes talking. He recognised one of them as his mother Rubia.

'What about Blackberry?' he heard her say. 'Has he spoken?'

Rubic decided to sleep a little longer.

Foxes brought him food. He vaguely recognised them, but they had been foxlings, really still cubs when he'd last seen them. None of them said much to him.

When eventually he had no excuse not to sit up and take notice of the world, another fox arrived. It was his father.

'We had a message you were nearly here,' said Black. 'A green bird brought it, so Brother Badger set out to find you. Welcome home, son.'

Rubic looked at his father.

'Really?' he said. 'I was supposed to go away, not come back.'

'Not true. The Running was to get your brother

Blackberry away and safe. You have done that. You have come back to tell us our story. Isn't that right?'

Gratitude and relief flowed through Rubic. He had so feared being unwelcome.

'It is winter,' said his father. 'Not that much to do. We will have a Talking, no, many Talkings and you can tell your tales to the tribe. Meanwhile,' went on this, the senior fox of the tribe, 'I think you had better do some eating. You look as if you need to.'

After that, everything got easier for Rubic. Rubia his mother came to see him and he told her of Blackberry's mate Rennet and their finding of their own den. He heard of her escape from the man she had bitten. That bite had ensured the escape of the seven and the beginning of the Running. She looked him up and down and from then on lots of little foxes came by with food of all kinds.

'Your mother says to try this,' was what they always said.

It was a cold winter. The snow lay for a month. The foxes gathered when and where they could. Not long after his mother's visit, one very early morning, as a pale winter sun began to rise and warm the land, Rubic found himself in front of a crowd of his tribe. In his audience was the tabby cat, whom he had been brought up to call Sister Cat, and also his rescuer, Brother Badger. He looked around for his grandmother Lucy, who had told so many stories and whose tales had given him answers in several of his adventures.

'Grandmother Lucy?' he said looking around.

There was a silence. It was Sister Cat who replied. Wild foxes never talk about ceasing to be.

'Gone to the ancestors,' she said.

Rubic too was silent for a moment, then he turned to his audience.

'Her stories saved me at least once,' he said. 'If she hadn't told us the story of Blackberry being cured by Brother Badger I wouldn't have known who to ask for help after the fight with the stoats and weasels.'

'Stoats and weasels?' said a young fox voice.

And so it began. Throughout the winter Rubic told his tales to his tribe. When Sister Cat was present he gave full credit to her near relations who had helped him and also told of the tigers he'd met, who were clearly felines, but rather more distant cousins.

Brother Badger heard about how in his fever Rubic had remembered his grandmother Lucy's words and sent George the magpie to find an Old One and call him Brother Badger, and how the badger had come and healed him.

'Hrmph,' said the cemetery badger. 'Causing my kind a lot of work aren't you?'

Eventually Rubic also talked about why he had left Devon, about being unable to kill to eat. There was much discussion. The foxes of the cemetery seemed more or less evenly divided between those who understood Rubic's point of view and felt the same and were happy to live on the city's debris and those who regarded a hunt with a fresh juicy rat or mouse at the end of it as a real treat.

Winter was long. Yet there came a morning when the foxes sniffed the air and felt a change. The next morning it was the same and the morning after. The year had turned. Spring was on its way.

By this time Rubic was once more a sleek fox. There was no way of repairing his torn ear but he was twice the weight he had been when he arrived in the cemetery. He was once again a glossy pale red and the beloved of the vixens. Many solicited his company but he responded rather half-heartedly.

The trouble was, now he was well and healthy, he remembered why the foxes had left the cemetery all that time ago. He remembered Blackberry saying that he wanted the moon to be free and not trapped in the trees. The cemetery and the streets felt like a cage. He thought wistfully of the Moor and its wide hillsides, of running with the deer and even of the big water, the seaside where Butch and Pearl had made their home. Spring was here and he had itchy paws.

Family matters were beginning to occupy the Cemetery Foxes. There were dens to be dug or tidied. Cubs were born and had to be admired and fed. Rubic hadn't found himself a mate, though several vixens tried to convince him of his destiny. He was wandering further from the cemetery each day.

22. An Unexpected Encounter

One morning, when trotting over the Heath, which was as like the openness of the Moor as he could find in the city, Rubic heard a noise he recognised.

It was the jangling of an electric organ. He followed the sound. He could see a fairground and a circus big top in the distance across the Heath. Soon he was sneaking under ropes and between tents. He wasn't sure what he was seeking, but felt compelled to search.

He heard a 'quark.'

He realised what he had been looking for. It was a friend. He crept under the flysheet of a large tent and found himself in the circus ring, under the Big Top. Sure enough, there in the ring, rehearsing their act, Rubic saw a young girl in glittering costume, a number of small yellow and blue birds and a large magpie with glowing iridescent azure and white wing patches.

The fox gave a quiet bark. He saw George's head turn and knew the magpie had heard. Rubic settled down to watch and wait.

George had got very good at what he did. He was now obviously completely part of the act. The little yellow birds rode on his head. He carried the little cart, he walked up the young girl's arm and took his bow sitting on her shoulder.

Eventually the rehearsal was finished. The little yellow birds were back in their cage and George perched on the cart as the girl wheeled the paraphernalia of the act from the ring.

Rubic followed, sneaking from cover to cover, from tent flap to tent flap. One of the caravans on the outskirts of the fair belonged to the girl. Rubic watched as George hopped onto a perch outside the door and the girl went into the van, taking the cage of budgerigars with her.

The fox slid under the caravan and waited. After a little while George joined him.

'Had to make sure she had settled in,' he said. 'Well? Did it all work out? Have you found your heart's desire?'

Rubic put his paws over his nose and shut his eyes. He wasn't sure where to start.

'This works for me,' went on the magpie. He

chattered on because he could see his friend wasn't ready to talk. 'There was some suggestion at the beginning that they should clip my wings and chain me to the perch, but she stopped them. She said I arrived of my own free will and she was sure I'd die if they did any such thing.' He paused and looked at Rubic. 'So I am a free bird but I've found another two-legged to love.'

Rubic couldn't tell the story of all his failures, of how none of his dreams had come true. He had been telling stories all winter to his tribe, but these had been of his adventures, not his feelings. George understood. He disappeared and came back with a bit of cold burger.

'Here, supper,' he said. 'They all feed me round here.'

The pair sat under the caravan in silence for a while. Gradually Rubic managed to put into words his disappointments. He told how the deer weren't free.

'Not so different from those rabbits when we found them,' said George.

He told of coming home and his anxieties, but how the tribe had welcomed him and now how he was feeling bad because he had become discontented with their life, the city life.

'Why can't I be happy? Find a good vixen, a den and cubs? What is wrong with me?'

'You simply haven't found your place yet,' said the bird.

It was several days before Rubic returned to

Highgate Cemetery. There was a freedom in the traveller camp: so much to see and watch in a circus, so many new creatures to talk to. He heard of their journeys up and down the land, of setting up in new places.

He talked to the horses who paraded with plumes upon their heads. He had always regarded horses as like canines, slaves of the two-leggeds. He was surprised at their independence and the stories they had to tell. One of them remembered Annie the elephant and so Rubic was able to pass on news of her.

There were many new foods to try. He made himself very sick eating a pink fluffy concoction, but developed a taste for riding on the Ferris wheel.

'You can see so far,' he said. 'My cousin Pearl, she flew with a Richard. It must have been a bit like this.'

George the magpie was, of course, unimpressed.

'Birds get much higher than that,' he said, but Rubic was pleased with his new view of the world.

The circus would be on the Heath for another month. The fox determined to return at least once more before it left for the summer.

When, almost a week later, he slipped through the iron railings back at the cemetery, he found his mother waiting in rampant mood.

'Where have you been? What have you been up to? We have been looking for you.'

He felt like a badly behaved cub again. He turned his back on her and disappeared off into the undergrowth. It was in the depths of the bushes, behind the statue of the big man, that the Badger found him.

'Hrmmph, they need you. There is a problem. There is a new cub. He is your nephew. He is like Blackberry. They say he needs to get away.' He paused. 'Things are changing in this place.'

Those few grunted words from Brother Badger summed up the situation among the Cemetery Foxes. All the meetings and conversations that followed changed nothing.

Rubia was this young one's great aunt. She was sure this cub must leave. She said so often, to all who would hear. That the new black cub had to go before he became a road casualty like Blackberry had and became another three-legged fox, or worse.

Other voices said a damaged fox was not a normal fox, and would have no place in the tribe. They didn't actually say that a black fox had no place in the cemetery at all. No amount of 'Well, Blackberry has done alright,' from Rubic made any difference.

Rubic went to look at this new cub. He was one of a litter of four. The other three were properly red, though one was rather a pale fox. That one reminded Rubic of himself. The little black cub was by this time four weeks old and though still mostly dependent on his mother's milk he was beginning to show he had a mind of his own.

'I can't keep him in,' said his mother, who was a

vixen cousin Rubic vaguely remembered. She was called Melissa and liked honey, but as he recalled it hadn't made her sweeter. She hadn't ever been a kind fox.

'He already is trying to wander off,' Melissa went on. 'He's not right. We city foxes aren't that colour. He must go.'

'We are what we are,' said Rubic. 'Anyway, what about my father?'

'He was born a long time ago. We're not dark like that now.'

Rubic didn't know what to make of this, so he went to see his mother. He told her what Melissa had said.

'What's it all about? He asked.

Her reply was unrelated to his question.

'You aren't going to stay are you? You haven't found a vixen. We aren't good enough for you.'

'What has that got to do with what that Melissa said? What I do is my affair.'

'Don't you see? Your father's time as Leader is coming to its end. He is old now. He will join the ancestors before too long. These new foxlings aren't into weird like you and Butch, or the dark colour. They think all foxes should be red.'

'So? That is just rubbish. We exist. We are.'

'Not if they can help it.'

Rubic didn't see the big picture. He didn't get what his mother was saying. He was more interested in his own pain. He wanted to talk about the past.

'But what about you, mother? You had favourites too. You never felt for Butch and me like you did for Blackberry.'

'Butch wasn't my cub, he was my sister's,' she said. 'I just had him in my den because she had gone to the ancestors.'

'And me?'

'I couldn't help it. Blackberry was a lovely cub. He was so clever. I just did love him so much and then he was damaged and then got better. You and Butch and Flutes were there to save him.'

Rubic was silent.

'Anyway,' said Rubia. 'None of that matters now. Don't be so sorry for yourself. Don't you see? This is bigger than you.'

But Rubic's thoughts stayed where they were.

'Blackberry was our leader on the Running,' he said. 'He was wise about things.' He looked accusingly at his mother and went on. 'He was wise because he was loved. He knew he had value.'

The mother fox looked impatiently at this difficult son, no longer a cub.

'For goodness sake. Do stop that. The past is the past. Will you listen? Your father's time as Leader is nearly over. They, the upcomers, are going to change the rules. That cub will die.'

'What do you mean?'

'He is different. They won't let him survive. Do you want to be part of a tribe that kills its own? You won't even kill your supper.'

'That Melissa doesn't like him, does she?'

'That is another reason he must go soon. She's his mother and if she won't fight for him ... We must get him away. Make a new story for him.'

Finally Rubic understood. Whatever issues he had with his mother, she had taught him her values. She and Black and Lucy his grandmother had led the tribe for years before he was born. They had, he knew, been good years and years when the Words had been respected. All foxes had known them. In the cemetery, all creatures were welcome at a Talking. Sister Cat and Brother Badger, squirrels and birds would regularly have their say.

He realised that the change of flavour in the tribe was one of the things that had made him wander. Family Values seem to be becoming Fox Values. Respect for other creatures was vanishing. He stood up and looked at his mother.

'I will go and talk to some friends,' he said. 'I think I know what to do. We have a week or two before he is weaned don't we?'

'Not longer though,' said Rubia. 'It would be so easy for them. But I will watch him.'

23.
AN ENDING?

The following day found Rubic deep in conversation with George the Magpie. The two were under the caravan where George's new friend and her birds lived. The posters called her 'Ruxandra, the Romanian Bird Whisperer'.

There was plenty of space beneath the van. It made a good den for Rubic while George perched on the gas cylinder low down at the back so they were able to have a sensible uninterrupted discussion.

'The cemetery is changing,' said Rubic. 'It's foxes forever and only red foxes at that. I couldn't understand why I wasn't happy being home, but I do now. There are lots of creatures under the sky. The fun is meeting them all. Not just sticking to one kind.'

'You know me,' said George. 'I could never be happy in a Tiding. I was reared by a two-legged. I know about natural mothers throwing you out.'

'My mother thinks this little black one's natural mother wants him gone. What to do?'

'You could bring him here,' said George. 'You'll have to. You can't let them disappear him. We'll manage. After all, oddities are what a circus is made of. That is why the grockles pay to see us.'

'Us, is it?' said Rubic.

'Yes, us,' said George. He was a little defiant. 'This is my place now.'

The fox pondered. It was a thought.

'But then ...' said Rubic. 'He's so young.'

'Travel with us. If he can't run, he can ride, on the vans. There is plenty of food.'

A decision seemed to have been made.

Rubic went back to the cemetery. As he wandered down the hill he heard sounds of yelping and anger. He rushed through the fence, down the wide avenue, towards the statue of the big man, where the sound was coming from.

He could see his mother backing towards the pink granite plinth of Lenin's memorial, snarling as she went. He could see a group of yearling foxes, not a single one of them as big as she was, but they were a pack and they were advancing with determination.

Rubic charged past the pack, onto the pink gravel. He turned and was side by side with his mother. He too snarled at the oncoming pack while he tried to work out what on earth was going on. Rubia barked to him:

'They came to get him. I took him. They want

him. Look.'

Rubic looked behind her and saw a pathetic little black bundle, huddled against the base of the statue. It didn't seem conscious.

'He got bitten,' said Rubia. 'They shan't have him.'

'I've found somewhere,' said Rubic.

'You take him. Now. Go.'

She said 'Go' as she had, once before, when a young one needed a rescue. 'I'll keep them busy.'

Rubic did what his mother told him. He grabbed the cub, in his jaws, by the scruff of the neck and slipped quickly behind the big statue. He still knew this ground better than most. He had been born here after all. Carrying the cub he dodged in and out of the graves, down narrow alleys and under a stone arch. Finally, he made it through the railings.

As he ran he could hear his mother's snarling interrupted. The pained yelp of another fox followed. Had he been human and not had his mouth full of foxcub he would have smiled.

'That'll teach them,' was his thought. 'She's not a fox to be messed with.'

He ran on and on, over the Heath. He dared not stop. He was afraid of pursuit. The cub wasn't a featherweight either. Rubic was pretty well exhausted by his burden when he skidded to a halt outside the caravan where George, his Romanian two-legged girl and the budgerigars lived.

He dropped the little black bundle on the grass and flopped down himself. George, on his perch, gave a startled quark. He hopped down to look.

The quark, however, had also been heard within the van. The door opened and Ruxandra stood at the top of the steps.

There was an odd sight in front of her. Anyone else would have assumed the pathetic pile of black fur was the prey of the magpie and the pale red fox, but this girl knew her creatures. She could see concern in George's gestures and exhaustion in Rubic. She realised he had carried this burden some distance.

She went down the caravan steps and, sitting on the bottom one, put her hand out to the little black bundle.

Rubic growled and backed away, but not very determinedly. George looked at the fox, croaked and shook his head. Rubic stayed still.

The girl withdrew her hand from the little fox cub and saw blood on it. She spoke in her own language.

'Oh, my little Negruskic. What has happened to you?'

She picked him up, cradled him in her arms and turned to go up the van steps.

'Oy, Roxy. What you got there?'

The male voice came from nearby and startled Rubic. He shot under the caravan.

Roxy, as she was known to all in the circus, still struggled with her English.

'Pup,' she said. 'Broke. I will mend.'

'Not a bad idea,' said the voice. 'You could do with a dog, you could. Living alone like that.'

It was so easily settled.

If Roxy knew she had a wild fox living under her caravan she never gave a hint of it, though perhaps she was inclined to be less tidy with her food scraps. George kept Rubic informed as to the cub's progress.

'He's coming on. Doing nicely. She calls him her Negruskic so that is his name, I think.'

Three weeks later the big top was taken down and the circus packed up. As the procession of vans and trucks made its way north to the next venue, no one except George the magpie knew that on the roof of Roxy's wagon, in between the bundles of props, lay Rubic, the fox who couldn't find his destiny.

Within the wagon, the budgies, the Magpie and the little black fox cub all managed to live with their mistress. There were adventures in front of them, but it would be some time before either of the two foxes or the Magpie managed to tell their story to their fellow creatures.

AfterWords

That winter was a hard winter on the High Tor. It was as well that Rubic had left. In the spring the new cubs were born. Flutes mothered and Blackberry fathered four cubs apiece. There were more young than there had been for many, many years. Most amazing of all was the litter that Elphine produced. She had no mate, but as Flora had said, Rubic had left something on the High Tor. She had two cubs, a boy and a girl. The boy was a good red fox colour like his mother but the girl was white. She was called Ruby after her father. It was felt she would be a good hunter in the winter snows.

A year later, in the June after she had had her second litter, as an experienced mother, Flutes found she had time to have a thought. She went to Blackberry. He looked at her.

'I was thinking the same thing,' he said.

'Troy's words,' said Flutes, 'until the Mela.'

'Yes,' said Blackberry. 'You're right. It is time.'

Thus it was the Foxes of High Tor called a Mela for the night of Samhain. That is the night the two-leggeds call Halloween. As the months went by, messages reached every corner of the fox world.

They made the Mela and it was splendid. Everyone came. It remains to this day part of creature legend. The story of the Running and Rubic's Return was spread far and wide. In every earth, in the dark of winter, when it was cold and all were snuggled up for warmth, the stories were told and retold. Among the newer stories was that of Butch's Island and Pearl the flying fox. There were other tales too, about other adventures and maybe they will be written down one day.

It remains true, as Black had said to the Cemetery Foxes, 'If we do not retell our stories, our history, we shall no longer be.'

THE END

Notes on the Creature Code and Foxtalk

The Creature Code for Interspecies Negotiations

These ancient words and phrases are used for interspecies communication. The responses and replies vary slightly from region to region, the intonation, however, remains constant. The code is universally observed and almost never violated. The most commonly used words and phrases are:

Pax: The truce greeting word to which the reply is 'Fainites'. The creatures may have taken these words from London children's playground games

in the 1950s.
Cheers Mate: The universal phrase meaning thankyou and goodbye.

Other phrases in use:
Good speed and a safe haven
A safe run and good speed.
There is room at the end of the line.

The Song

Rainbow, rainbow, rainbow too
Sun comes back for me and you.

This is 'the song that is never sung', i.e. the same promise that Noah understood. Rubic reminds Buckfast of its significance. In the rabbit tribe at Stonehenge it had degenerated to a skipping game.

Foxtalk

These phrases are peculiar to the foxes and not universal.
'We'll meet again': the unspoken addition is 'with the ancestors' i.e. after death.
'Until the Mela': A phrase revived by Troy, the equivalent of 'au revoir'.

The Foxes rhyming slang is mostly used in naming each other and is possibly derived from its cockney equivalent:

Rubic – Ruby Murray – curry, but for a male it becomes Rubic.
Butch – butcher's hook – look.
Pearl – girl

The other foxes who did the Great Running with Blackberry were:
Flutes – bossy boots
Troy – boy
Piana – Joanna

Other Words Used in the Books

Richard – Richard III – bird.
Mela: originally a sanscrit word for a fair, a gathering. There are Mela all over India. Foxes 'make a Mela'. The London two-leggeds' Mela in 2012 was in Gunnersbury Park, West London.
Samhain: Halloween night, 31st October. The word is perhaps taken from Celtic foxtalk. There were black foxes in Wales, who might once have brought the word to London.

Natural History and Geographical Trivia

Foxes (Vulpes vulpes)

The Fox doesn't, as far as I know, communicate with other species, though there is a film of a cat rearing fox cubs in the 1930s. However, the fox behaviours detailed in the text are as far as possible based on personal observation and research.

Melanistic (black) and albino (white) foxes though rare, do exist. Professor Google will give photos and film of a black fox in Hounslow, London. A hunters' website has a film of two white foxes shot in Kent.

Foreign fur fox escapees are reported in the countryside though they usually do not survive for long. Foxes do eat blackberries.

Red Deer (Cervus elaphus)

The largest native deer, found all over northern Europe. They are common on Dartmoor, but a great deal easier to see in Richmond Park, where an observer may get up to within ten feet of a stag.

The Red Deer of Richmond Park

It is only deer – not human – legend that the Richmond Park Red deer are descended from the Dartmoor red deer, but red deer were referred to in 1920 by Archibald Thorburn, a well-known 19C wildlife artist as 'the grandest wild animal of Britain' and it is hard to challenge that. The Celts called them fairy deer and have many tales of people changing into deer and the reverse.

Cobbett in 1826, when arguing against the protection of deer in the New Forest, asks 'What are deer for? Who are to eat them? Are they for the Royal Family? Why there are more deer bred in Richmond Park alone ... than would feed all branches of the Royal Family and all their households all the year round.' He regarded deer as 'another deep bite into us by the long and sharp-fanged aristocracy'.

The grave of the king that the red deer of Richmond Park consider they are guarding is that of James IV of Scotland who was killed at the battle of Flodden in 1513. His body is said to have been brought to England and buried in the monastery at Sheen, which then was in Rich-mond Park. A memorial stone may be found at the site of the Abbey on the local golf course.

Fallow Deer (Dama dama)

'The Frenchies.' This is what the red deer of Richmond Park call the fallow deer. Fallow deer are non-indigenous and said to have been brought to England by William the Conqueror. These are the smaller deer in Richmond Park.

In this tale, if they communicate, they do it in ancient French and still have a recognisable French accent.

However, there is a suggestion that an earlier population of fallow deer came over with the Romans in the first century, and some accompanied Joseph of Arimathea to Glaston-bury. The deer were said to be with him the night he stuck his staff in the ground and fell asleep on the Tor.

The next morning, the staff had grown into the famous Glastonbury Thorn, but St Joseph woke to see his deer browsing on the miraculous tree. He was so angry he banished them from Somer-set to the darkness of the Forest of Dean. The forest deer have darker hides than the London fallow deer and have a different voice. They are very clear that their English heritage is a thousand years older than that of the Richmond Park newcomers, the 'Frenchies'.

The Others

Badgers (Meles Meles)

The badgers maintain they are the oldest inhabitants of the kingdom. They say they were there before the stones of Stonehenge were erected. This is true. Badgers kin may well have walked with dinosaurs, in China at least. Fossils 250,000 years old have been found there.

In England until 18C, they were known as Brock, meaning grey, from the Celtic.

They are social animals, usually living in families but also have been known to share an earth/sett with foxes. In a cold winter they sleep a lot and are notoriously angry if disturbed.

Brown Rat (Rattus Norvegicus)

This species arrived in the UK in the eighteenth century and used to be known as the Hanover rat. It congregates in large numbers and is often quoted as the most successful creature on the planet. It can swim.

It has been misnamed norvegicus. The rat was found in the UK long before it reached Norway.

It is the rat of Robert Browning's Pied Piper of Hamlyn, though that legend of stolen children dates back to the thirteenth century.

Cat (Felis cattus)

This is the shorthaired domestic cat of no particular breed. The writer's ideal cat is Rudyard Kipling's 'The cat that walked by himself.'

Manx Cats

Manx cats are descended from the African wild cat (*Felis silvestris lybica*). They come in all colours, just like any domestic cat, but have no tail.

Noah is said to have closed the door of the ark on a cat's tail and thus the first Manx cat came into being. In fact, they are now a recognised breed, the product of a genetic abnormality. Each Manx cat can only have one dose of the tailless gene. A double dose is lethal, thus two Manx cats never successfully produce tailless offspring. They have been exhibited since the 1800s.

They are well known for being good ratters. It is probable that Dick Whittington's cat was Manx.

Cabbit is a term of abuse in the cat world. It implies a liar. The term came about as it was surmised by humans that the original Manx cats were a cross between a cat and a rabbit. Both cats and rabbits know this is a myth and are suitably scornful, thus in both cat and rabbit speak a Cabbit is a liar and untrustworthy.

Rabbits (Oryctolagus cuniculus)

They are said to have been discovered in Spain by the Phoenicians. 'Hispania' is also said to be a corruption of a Phoenician term meaning 'Land of Rabbits'. When the Romans reached Spain in second century BC they realised the potential of the species and began to farm them. Thus they arrived in England and the rest of the then-known world with the Legions. In England, they were kept in warrens, which was roughly equivalent to keeping free range hens today. The creatures were uncaged but lived in a dug pit enclosed by a ditch within which was a big burrow, a 'pillow mound'. They were harvested when required. This does mean that perhaps all English wild rabbits can trace their ancestry back to relatives who escaped from Roman warrens. Pope Gregory (540–604 AD) declared that it was allowable to eat foetal or new-born rabbits (laurices) during Lent and on fast days when meat wasn't allowed, provided the doe wasn't killed. Warrens then became common in monasteries. This casts a new light on the idea of the Easter Bunny!

Bats

(Order: Archonta, which includes primates and lemurs; then Chiroptera, which means 'hand wing')

Bats aren't rodents. There are about eighteen species of bat in the UK. Most are very rare. The most often found is the Common Pipestrelle (Pipestrellus pipestrellus) and these were the cloud of bats Rubic and George met on the church roof. They are tiny (1.25 in./4 cm).

Bats are nocturnal. They may eat 3000 insects a night. In other parts of the world, bats pollinate night-flowering plants like cocoa, thus Gabrielle's statement that we owe chocolate to bats.

There are many folktales about them. In Nigeria, the bat is believed to be nocturnal because he is hiding from hunters who want to capture him for causing the death of his friend, the bush rat. The Arabs, the Polish and the Chinese consider bats bring longevity and happiness. In Tonga, they are sacred.

Their image is to be found on lots of shields and football club pennants in Spain. They are known as 'cave chicken' and eaten in Indonesia and the Pacific Rim, where they are much bigger of course!

Amur Tiger (Tigris altaica)

The Amur tiger is also known as the Siberian tiger and at the moment is regarded as an endangered species but with a stable population. Their natural habitat is the Russian Far East. In the wild population, there has been found to be very little genetic diversity. It is estimated at 500.

The worldwide captive 'reserve' population consists of about 450 tigers, most of whom were born in zoos etc. and are all descended from 85 captured individuals. For these 450 tigers there is now a stud book, and breeding among them is carefully controlled to ensure as much genetic diversity as possible.

This explains the sadness among the tigers in this tale. They aren't considered suitable to breed from, so they are fed contraceptives. Since beginning this story, the writer has learnt that Turlough, the Amur tiger, born in captivity in 1996, died at Longleat in June 2013.

Indian Elephant (Elephas Maximus)

When the writer worked in a remote bit of southern Africa and told local people that in some countries elephants didn't just cause trouble by trampling crops and bumping into cars, but actually worked, they were incredulous. On leaving the country for India, I sent a lot of postcards of working Indian elephants to Africa.

Indian elephants are recorded as war elephants from earliest times. Hannibal famously took elephants across the Alps in 217 BC. More recently, Oliver Reed walked his animal to Switzerland during World War II in the film Hannibal Brooks. The film was loosely based on a true story as many zoo animals were moved in the Second World War to avoid allied bombing.

Circus elephants have always been Indian elephants. They have been on display in menageries since Roman times and have performed in circuses since circuses began. Alexander the Great brought the first Indian elephants through the Hindu Kush to Europe.

Hansken, a female Indian elephant, toured Europe and was sketched by Rembrandt in 1637.

Anne, the elephant encountered by Rubic, is indeed the last elephant to have performed in a circus in England and is indeed living out her retirement at Longleat.

The Weasel Family (Mustelidea)

The mustelidae, in evolutionary terms are descended from the wolf-like vulperines.

Ferrets (Mustela Furo)

The ferret is the domesticated European polecat. They have been domesticated for at least 2500 years and may well have come to the UK with the Romans, like the rabbits. Ferreting, the hunting of rabbits in their burrows was their main use.

They happily coexist and breed with polecats, their wild equivalent. They are 9–18 in,/50 cm long (but about 5 in./13 cm of that is a tail) and weigh between 1 and 3 lb/0.7–2.0 kg. They vary in colour. Rex, the ferret in this story, was an albino with pink eyes, not a pure white, but a beige colour.

The stoat or ermine is said to be the creature in Leonardo da Vinci's picture 'Lady with an ermine', but given the size of the creature it looks like a ferret to me and very like the Rex in this story, who was based on a pet I once had.

Stoats (Mustela erminea)

The stoat is about 8–12 in./18.7–32.5 cm long. The Jacks (males) are often twice the size of the Jills (females). Males weigh about 9 oz/258 g and females 6.3 oz/180 g. In winter they turn completely white as camouflage in the snow. Sometimes, however, the snow doesn't come. The writer has seen a white stoat running around a Scottish glen, before the snow arrived. Stoats are carnivores and will tackle prey larger than themselves.

Their tails, with their black tips, were used for many years to trim academic and aristocratic robes.

Mythologically, they have a mixed press. It is unlucky to meet one when starting on a journey, in Ireland, but the ill luck may be diverted by greeting it as a neighbour. A white stoat was regarded as a symbol of purity in Christian Europe.

Weasels (Mustela nivalis)

Its official common British name is 'least weasel'. It is very similar to the stoat, but smaller, 5–9 in./12.7 cm long and has no black tip to its tail.

It is the smallest British carnivore. Its biology and breeding habits are different from stoats, but otherwise they are very alike, The weasel, lacking the black tail tip which deters predators is more often prey.

There are no 'least weasels' in Ireland. There is no record of whether they ever encountered St Patrick, like the snakes are said to have done.

Mythologically, views are mixed. In Greece, they are believed to destroy the wedding dresses of brides. An Inuit hero when about to embark upon an adventure would often transform himself into a weasel, but the Witchfinder General in 16C England regarded weasels as the familiars of witches.

The Birds

Buzzards (Buteo buteo)

The most common big hawk observed in English skies. These are the birds with wedge-shaped tails who glide low over fields and motorways.

Red Kites (Milvus milvus)

Another very large hawk and a rescue success story. These birds were nearly extinct but were supported in mid-Wales and now can be seen all down the M4 and M5 motorways. They eat carrion and are a sort of English vulture. Their flight pattern is quite different to that of the buzzard. They have forked tails and wheel and turn and swerve. The best comparison the writer can come up with is that the buzzard is a fixed wing, while the red kite is a hang glider.

Harris Hawks (Parabuteo unicinctus)

These hawks are commonly used in falconry displays. They are non-native, found, among other places, in America. The Harris hawk is the only hawk which hunts socially, because as a desert bird, hunting in groups, a group catches more prey. There are escapes. The writer regularly watches a Harris hawk which lives in a park in central Plymouth with a family of buzzards. There is now a young hybrid whose photo has appeared in the local paper. All these raptors spread alarm by swooping low over the small dogs exercising in the park and the pigeon population has decreased.

Ring-necked Parakeets (Psittacula krameri)

Though parakeets have been around London since Victorian times, they only began to breed in England in the late 1960s and are now considered naturalised. There are estimated to be perhaps 30,000 or more in the UK.

There are two urban legends as to their origins in London. A pair were said to have been released by Jimmy Hendrix. Alternatively some were said to have escaped from the set of the film The African Queen.

They are reported as preyed upon by the cities re-established raptors. Web cams have seen them as food in peregrine falcons' nests. Attitudes to them are inclined to be political. The Independent celebrates 'London's beautiful parakeets'. The Telegraph writes 'Noisy parakeets drive away native birds'.

Magpies (Pica pica)

The magpie is a member of the crow family. It is often seen taking eggs and nestlings from other birds' nests. During the 19C, it was much hunted for its plumage, but as this is no longer the case, it has greatly increased in numbers. Magpies are said to collect shiny objects, but this may be a myth. Their collective noun is a 'Tiding' of magpies.

A 19C fable existed that the Magpie was the only bird not to go into the Ark with Noah, but sat outside jabbering over the drowning world. Magpies are often seen as a bad omen. The rhymes, of which there are many, spoken when seeing a magpie, are said to be about warding off the devil.

Magpies mate for life and are the only birds

known to be able to recognise themselves in mirrors. They are said to attend funerals of their own kind.

The magpie is the national bird of Korea and well regarded there. A sighting is said to bring great good fortune.

London Feral Pigeons (Columba Livia domestica)

They are descended from escaped domestic pigeons and may well have come to England with the Romans. The first recorded complaint about them in London as feral is in the 14C when citizens were throwing stones at St Paul's, aiming to hit the pigeons, but ended up breaking the cathedral windows.

They are seen on wall paintings of 5000 years ago and Neolithic man, some 10,000 years ago, kept rock doves. All religions regard them with favour.

In more recent times, pigeons have run an airmail service in New Zealand between Auckland and Great Barrier Island, and were still used in Orissa, India, by the police as a messaging service until 2006 when email finally made them redundant. Reuters set up a pigeon carrier service in 1850, as pigeon mail was far faster than the then-current rail service.

The Dickon medal is the animal Victoria Cross. Pigeons have received 32, more than any other creature. Their stories are worth reading.

Feral pigeons make long-term though not

unbreakable pair bonds. They breed so successfully because they are largely independent of the weather. Squabs are fed on pigeon milk regurgitated by both parents, who also share egg incubation. Thus parents can convert discarded pizza etc. into infant food and are not dependent on seasonal insects or seeds. They can fly at 78 miles/126 km an hour.

One of the writer's sadder losses is the Christmas trip to Trafalgar square to see the giant Norwegian Christmas tree and feed the pigeons. There are now so very few pigeons there.

Greater Black-Backed Gull (Larus Marinus)

Is the largest of the seagulls seen in the UK and much larger than any of the others, having a five-foot/152 cm wingspan. Individuals have been recorded as living 25 years or more. They will defend their nests. The writer has been dive-bombed by one on Lundy Island when inadvertently venturing too near. They are formidable.

Mute Swans (Cygnus olor)

The indigenous UK swan is the white mute swan. They mate for life if they can, but will find a new partner if the first is lost. Their cygnets are brownish like Hans Anderson's Ugly Duckling but a few cygnets carrying a particular gene are born white and known as 'Polish' swans.

Black Swans (Cygnus astratus)

The black swan is Australian, but is almost considered a naturalised British species. It is found in many locations in the UK. It has interbred with the mute swan in captivity.

Flora

Truffles (Tuber ascomycete aestivum)

Truffles are fungi which grow at the base of certain trees and feed on their roots. They are much prized in the human world. In the creature kingdom, they are known as Earth Eggs. They have a very potent smell which is attractive to sows as it resembles the smell of the boar. There is a superstition that they are a remedy for male infertility.

They have been around a long time and were valued by the ancient Amorites who lived where Syria is today. Around 2000 BC their neighbours the Sumarians described them with contempt as a people who live in draughty tents, wander about the desert and dig up truffles to eat.

Since then, as food, truffles have gone in and out of favour. In Medieval times, the Church regarded them as 'witches' fare'. In 19C in France they were prized and attempts to cultivate them began. From the 1700s onwards, truffle hunting was a cottage industry in England. Individual truffle hunters such as Eli Collins became well known in 19C. Specially bred dogs were used. A truffle hound was usually a poodle/terrier cross with a thick curly coat to protect it in undergrowth.

In 1860, a dog tax of 12/- a year was introduced which made keeping a dog simply for truffle-hunting uneconomic for most villagers. The First World War also played its part in the decline of truffles. After 1918, there were far fewer men in need of a supplementary rural income to do the hunting. A wander through Google will demonstrate how interest in truffles has revived in recent times.

Should you believe in them, Ley lines are said to be good truffle hunting places.

The chocolate truffle is so named because the French chef Escoffier thought it resembled the real thing.

Mushrooms and Toadstools generally

Though no fungi other than truffles, which have to be dug up rather than picked, are mentioned in this story, it is worth saying that only a very few fungi or toadstools are seriously poisonous to humans. The trouble is that these have a nasty habit of looking like the common field mushroom.

All fungi collection should only be undertaken with guidance. In France, pharmacists will identify any wild mushrooms collected and declare them edible or dangerous.

Richmond Park

The King's Mound in Richmond Park is said to be where Henry VIII watched for the signal from the tower that his second wife, Anne Boleyn, had been executed. It is a legend, as he was known to be elsewhere at the time, but the fact remains that from the Mound, any two-legged, especially with the aid of the telescope provided, can see St Paul's Cathedral some ten miles/sixteen kilometres away in the centre of the City. The view is protected by laws and thus is a place of pilgrimage far older than the Wyche Tree, whose days nature had clearly numbered.

The grave of James IV of Scotland, killed in battle on English soil has indeed been lost, but there is now a plaque on the golf course adjoining the Park, recording the fact.

Avalon Weston

Avalon Weston was a midwife and began writing fiction rather late in life. She has, to date, published a detective story and three children's books. Her latest venture is to edit her great aunt's World War One diaries. 'Gabrielle West was such a lively person, taking her dog and her bicycle everywhere and watching Zeppelins bomb London, that I felt the diaries deserved a wider audience and now exist as a resource for anyone researching that period. History was fun, but I'm glad to get back to producing fiction.'

22439142R00150

Printed in Great Britain
by Amazon